FINDING ROSIE

a novel

W.B. EDWARDS

In loving memory of Marge and Burt Millen, both of whom helped me in so many ways over the years. RIP

And to all of the proud women of Olongapo City who gave of their love and lives while maintaining their dignity, during the Vietnam war.

The Sea, The Waves, and The Fish
(1965)

Part one: California
(1973)

Part two: The P.I.
(1969–1971)

Part three: The Old Man in the Restaurant
(1973)

THE SEA, THE WAVES, AND THE FISH

The dark morning sky felt heavy and humid, making it a little hard to breath. The sun had made the smog seem even thicker than usual that day, but now at four in the cool morning Paul Sutton was ready. He stood waiting in the front yard of his parents' house, waiting for his best friend Don Frank to come. Paul was glad to be going, it would be an adventure.

It will be good to get away, he thought. School would start soon, his first year at the new Junior College, and he'd have to probably work weekends and some nights, and so there wouldn't be much time for surfing. Paul sighed. Without going to college he'd get drafted for sure. That would be no fun. That would be fucked. One of his older friends had been drafted just weeks ago, and was now in boot camp at Fort Ord. Paul got scared just thinking about that, about having to go to Army boot camp, much less being in the war. He didn't understand or care about the war in Viet Nam.

But now, in the darkness of the morning, there came two bright white headlights down his street. The pavement shown gray under them, and the trees lit up overhead, and Paul could hear the thin whine of the gears, and he knew it was Don Frank in his white Volkswagen bus.

The van pulled up in front of the house and in the darkness he and Don loaded the surfboards on the rack on top. Don tied the boards down, and then the two looked at one another in the darkness.

"Let's go," said Don.

Paul laughed. "All Right!"

And with the radio playing softly and the heater warming their bare feet, they were off. It wasn't until they were well out of town and heading south on the long, and at this hour lonely and exciting Pacific Coast Highway, that the sun began to rise, spreading its golden glow and promised warmth over the hills to the east. The sky turned clear and blue and it promised to be a perfect summer day. They rolled along as the sun rose higher, and the white van caught the sun and threw a bright reflection at cars that passed. They turned inland, and then south again, and eventually passed into San Diego. The city was quiet in the morning sun. They headed into Ocean Beach for some breakfast at the Village Townhouse on Newport Avenue. The surf looked pretty small as they drove by.

Don Frank stayed here with his Aunt during the summer months, or at least he had until this year. He stayed with his mother up in Santa Monica during school and went to the same high school as Paul, which was how they knew each other and had become friends, but Don had always been down here in Ocean Beach during the summers, and now that school was out he'd likely be moving down here permanently. He liked it better, he said. It was more laid back, he said. Not like L.A. The little beach town just seemed funky to Paul, but he'd been here a few times with Don and he knew they had good surfing.

Then they were in Mexico. Baja looked dried up and brown, once they got past the streets of Tijuana and into the country. The sun seemed to beat down on the land, on the road, on their little van. They rolled down the front windows and Paul took off his t-shirt.

"I can't wait to get in that ocean," said Don.

"I just hope the surf is good," answered Paul. He hadn't been down to Baja before, but Don had come several times before, with his father. His Dad didn't surf but liked to camp and fish, and that was the only time he spent with his son.

"Yeah. You're gonna like this reef, man. It's so secret, so never crowded. Awesome right-hand tubes!" Don laughed his funny laugh, almost a cackle.

"I guess if it's no good, it'll still be worth this trip," Paul said, looking out the window at the changing scenery. "How much longer?"

"We're almost to Ensenada, it's not far after that."

"Well, I guess I'll try to sleep for awhile."

Paul put his head back against the seat and closed his eyes. The sun was in his face, but it felt good and he relaxed. But he couldn't sleep. His mind swam with thoughts and pictures. He tried to picture how the surf would be, but he was sure that he would be disappointed. And then a mental picture came that did something inside of him. Blue eyes and dark hair and very white skin, with odd brown little freckles. Kathy. His high school sweetheart. Gone to Hawaii. Would he ever see her again? He tried to put her out of his mind, but the picture remained. He could almost smell her. But the sun came red through his eyelids, and the soft heat was relaxing, and it emptied his mind of her for a while.

"There it is!" exclaimed Don Frank loudly. Paul came awake startled. He looked about as if he were lost, and then the ocean, shining and blue, was filling the windshield and his eyes, and as his awareness of where he was and that he'd been sleeping came to him, it made him laugh aloud.

They had to pay a few US dollars, but then they had their own camping spot for a week. Don parked the van, and they were out and running for the sand. But when they came up to the top of the little hill where they could see the surf breaking out on the reef, they stopped. The tide was out, and half the rocky reef was exposed, but the waves weren't breaking.

"Oh bitchin," said Don Frank.

They sat together in the back of the van with the door open and faced the sunset red and golden over the sea. The sand was yellow and almost gold now and there was a bright path of orange and gold down the middle of the ocean. The sun was very bright just above the horizon. They had eaten some sandwiches brought from home, and now sat drinking Corona beers and smoking Winston's, and the smoke curled up slowly in the windless air. The sea was nearly silent.

"We could have gone up north instead," said Don.

"There probably isn't any swell up there either," said Paul.

"Yeah. Maybe we should have just stayed home then."

"It's too close to school starting. College starting. I'd be going nuts at home."

"Hmm," said Don.

"And you can never tell about the waves."

"The tide will be pretty high in the morning."

"We'll just have to wait and see. Hope it's at least rideable"

"Yeah."

"Maybe we should go back into town and get really drunk, "said Paul.

"We don't have enough money to do that. It's all about food and gas." Don said. Then he said, "But there's a little market and stuff back up the hill there at the turn-off. We can walk up there and get some more beers or some wine maybe."

And so, they locked up the van and walked through the campground and up the road from the sea in the sunset.

The little market was about to close when they got there. Inside was a tubby little brown man who was sweating, and there were little beads of sweat on his face and his little dark mustache. But he smiled warmly at them, showing a row of brown yellow teeth, and took their money for another six pack of beer, a bottle of cheap red wine, and a bag of ice. The boys walked back down the hill to the camp in the darkness. Stars filled the sky. It was never like that back in L.A. Nobody in the camp seemed to be asleep, and yellow lights shown in the tents and campers all around the van.

"Let's get drunk," said Don Frank, and he and Paul laughed and they got paper cups, filling them with ice and poured in the warm red wine. They were sitting again in the back of the van with the door slid open to the night air.

Paul took a first timid sip of his wine. It wasn't cold enough yet and he shuddered at the taste. He'd never been a real fan of wine, but back in high school that was what they usually could get their hands on. Drinking at night under the high school bleachers.

"What's it like?" asked Don.

"Oh, it's good, it's real good. Just like any red wine I've had before." Paul hated it.

Don drank about half his cup down. "Not bad," he said, but his face twisted up.

"Well, let's drink this stuff and get it over with," said Paul.

After the first two cups the bottle did not look so scary and tasted better, and the night was getting warmer and friendlier and the wine was not so sour anymore. Then the ice was gone and they were drinking it warm, but now the taste was warm and friendly as the night itself. There was little talk now between them, as if it might disturb something.

When the big jug of a bottle was empty they felt warm and dizzy and tired. They went down to the water to relieve themselves, pissing into the sand, then they put their feet in the water and let it wash over their ankles, then they went to sleep in the van. Later, in the middle of the night, Paul awoke to the sound of crashing heavy surf, but he knew it had to be a dream, so he turned over and went back to sleep.

The morning came cold foggy and wet. Paul came awake as if he had not really been sleeping, and somehow, he knew it was near seven o'clock. He sat up in his sleeping bag and looked out through the rear window of the van. The sight of the fog made him feel cold. He looked over at Don, but there was only a big lump in the green sleeping bag. Paul crawled out of his sleeping bag and put his long pants on, then he went quietly out of the van's side door. The heavy sound of breaking surf seemed to make his stomach churn. That and the cold fog dampness made him feel a little sick, and he regretted the wine last night. But he knew he couldn't go back to sleep, so he had to wake up his friend.

"What?" said Don Frank.

"I said, surf's up! It came up huge,"

"What? Oh." Don didn't bother with his pants, he jumped out just wearing his trunks and last night's t-shirt. "Foggy," he said.

They stood listening to the waves breaking out on the reef. Paul could imagine how they were forming, gray and slick in the fog, and the white water cold and powerful in the morning.

The water was cold. There was a light wind blowing on Paul's back as he knee-paddled out. They paddled next to each other, and on their knees to keep away from the water as long as possible. When Paul saw the first wave he couldn't believe it. Too perfect. Don said something loudly, but Paul paid no attention. The wave rolled along towards them, throwing out in a great curl from top to bottom away to their right. The curl came towards them fast, and they moved their arms in the water quickly to get over the wave's shoulder and outside. Paul wasn't tired, cold or sick anymore.

"Damn," said Don. "Did you see that wave!"

"Here comes another one!"

"Mine!" yelled Don. He sat quickly back on his board, swinging it around to point towards the beach, and was in the wave, his board hissing as he dropped down the face. Paul watched him ride from behind, hearing him yelling and hooting.

Then it was Paul's turn, and another perfect swell formed green and glassy and he caught it with only a few strokes, dropping straight down and off the bottom back up into the wave's face. Now he stepped forward on the board, picking up speed. He would need it. He could see the lip of the wave already beginning to curl over ahead of him. He didn't want to wipe out and have to swim on his first wave, but he took a chance. Crouching low to center his gravity, he sped under the breaking curl. He put his hands out in front of him and watched the slick vertical wall on his right begin to snap and spit over his head and shoulders and felt spray on his arms. He closed his eyes and left it to fate, thinking he wasn't going to make it. But then he was gliding out on the shoulder of the wave, into the clear water, where he could see the rocks underneath, and he stood up and turned out of the wave, dropping onto his belly to paddle out for another.

That night, just after the sun had gone down, Paul and Don sat again in the back of the van with the doors open. They shivered in the cool breeze with their still wet hair slick and shiny in the light from the van. They had just come out of the water for the third time and they were very tired. Tired but very happy. This was what they'd come for, and much better than they'd hoped. "If it's like that again tomorrow, I'll stay out all day," declared Paul

"Not paddle in, even for lunch?" Don had a sarcastic tone, but he grinned.

"Well, we did that today and I almost fell asleep after!"

"Hah!"

"Those waves were so perfect though."

"I know. Did you see the last ride I got? Outasight! Smaller, but I got five toes over forever."

Paul nodded, smiling his approval. "Yeah, I kept getting tubed, so perfect out there. And all to ourselves. Definitely outasight! Thanks for making me come down here ol' buddy!" And he slapped Don lightly on his back.

"Oh yeah," said Don, grinning.

Paul sighed. "I'm tired as hell. Let's eat and crash"

"Well, what do we eat? I'm sick of peanut butter sandwiches."

"Today deserves something better," said Paul. "Let's walk up into town again."

They got dressed and put on shoes and long pants with long sleeve shirts and headed up the hill towards the town. As they walked along an old man in a brown Ford pick-up truck with a white camper shell on its back stopped and offered them a ride. He was staying in the camp to fish off the rocky point, and he told them he knew a good place to eat, as that's where he too was going.

The little place where the old man took them was dark and warm and smelled of fried food and beer. For no reason he could think of, Don explained to the old man that they would have driven up themselves but were trying to save gas.

"I understand," said the old man, his blue eyes twinkling. Paul wondered how old he was and where he was from. He spoke without any accent, but his truck had Mexican plates.

They all had taquitos and beans and rice, and they were the big fat round taquitos stuffed with lettuce and green chilis and pork and were excellent.

"Have you had much luck fishing?" asked Paul.

"I haven't had the luck with fish as you boys seem to have had today with the waves. You were out there a long time today, since before the fog lifted."

"The waves were very good," said Don.

"Maybe tomorrow I will be luckier," said the old man. His eyes brightened.

"Well, when the waves are really good, you just can't get enough."

Paul and Don nodded together.

"Maybe tomorrow some halibut or mackerel," said the old man. "I only need to catch one or two big fish."

"Surfing is different," said Paul. "Just one good wave, that can almost seem like it would be enough, you know, thinking about it. But when you ride one good wave, you just want another one!" He laughed.

"I thought maybe it had to do with size, with how big the wave is," said the old man.

"Not really, not all the time anyway."

The old man drove the boys back down to the campground, and they thanked him and said they'd look for him tomorrow, and then they went happily to bed.

The next morning was the same, except there was no fog, only a gray overcast sky that made the glassy sea the same gray as itself. But the big kelp beds outside of the surf line were dark green and moved slowly in the swells, rising and falling.

Paul awoke and saw that Don was soundly sleeping and so he didn't wake him. He went quietly out of the van and saw that the surf was perfect again and decided to just go out alone. He'll wake up pretty soon anyway, he thought.

The water was still cold. But Paul lay flat on his belly and paddled out quickly with strong deep strokes of his arms. He thought the maybe the waves were a little smaller today. As he paddled he could see an old man sitting out on the rocks to his right, with his fishing line in the water.

Paul sat in the water and watched the swells as they formed up outside in the kelp beds and grew as they pushed in to the shallower water of the reef under him. The waves lifted him and then broke some twenty feet towards shore from where he sat on his board, waiting. He sat like that for what seemed like a long time, thinking about surfing. He thought of the feeling he had when he was inside a wave, really inside, and he thought of how it was when he came out again. He saw that he couldn't really capture the memory of it, not really. It was only inside that you knew.

Paul decided it was time now, and he took the very next wave that came. It was long and fairly fast, but for some reason Paul felt stiff and nervous and he found himself too high in the wave for too long, and he wiped out and had to swim for the board. Luckily it didn't go all the way inside to the really shallow water with the rocky bottom.

He had to wait a long time for the next wave, for there was a lull. The surf was not as consistent as it had been the day before. Paul wondered when Don would wake up. He paddled a little further out, not knowing why. It was just a feeling.

Now there came a large swell on the horizon, Paul thought it was bigger than any he'd seen so far. Maybe 8 or 10 feet. The wave came on, and it was moving very fast and Paul knew it would be hollow and fast breaking and that he had to take it, feeling the fear in his chest. He swung his board around and felt the sudden lift and had to paddle hard and fast. Now the wall of water fell away below him, green and slick, and he knew he had it. His board was headed downwards and going very fast as he jumped to his feet, planting them quickly as he dropped halfway down the face of the wave. Dropping the rest of the way down he made his turn a wide sweeping bottom turn, which carried him in one smooth movement back up into the curling wave face towards the lip, which had spray coming off in the off-shore breeze. He wasn't nervous or tight now, and there was a thing that wanted to burst in his chest, making him suddenly scream with joy. The wall of water was long in front of him, and just for a moment he drank in the beauty of the sparkling green surface. But he could also see that this wave was quickly hollowing out in front of him, too quickly for his position. He headed at an angle for the flat water out in front of the wave, picking up speed from his rapid descent, and turned to get back up into the face again. But he was sucked up higher than he wanted, so he stepped forward and crouched down, dropping down the face again, and the wave curled and spit and threw out over him, and he was inside the tube again. For maybe the first time ever he thought he could actually hear the crashing roaring sound the wave made, that seemed to come from it's very guts. He put his head down between his outstretched arms and closed his eyes. He hoped Don was up now to see this ride. Then the tunnel of water caught him and exploded all around him and threw him down hard onto the rocky bottom. He felt the surprising impact as his shoulder crashed into the rocks. Then blackness.

Paul's board washed up on the beach, but the old man on the rocks did not see it, for he was very busy with a big fish.

PART ONE

CALIFORNIA 1973

CHAPTER ONE

I t was November, and it was a typical gray, cloudy, windy, and cold day at the beach. Paul Sutton stood in the sand at Malibu beach in his bare feet and old Levi's and blue parka and watched cold gray-green little waves breaking along the rocky beach.

Just watching them made him shiver. A light mist began to drift down from the sky that he could feel hit his face. Maybe next summer, he thought. Maybe next summer I'll try and start surfing again. He was just too cold to think about it now. He wondered again how long it would take him to readjust to living here again, after the tropics.

A cold beer would be nice though, he thought, as he drove away from the beach and its wet sand in the little Chevy Nova. It was his girlfriend's car. Mary's.

There was a bar just off the Coast Highway that was not too far. He decided to go there. Mary wouldn't be home for a while anyway, he told himself.

It was a small bar and it was empty except for the bartender who did not bother to ask Paul for any identification. He poured out a tall glass of beer and set it on the counter in front of Paul. He watched him sip at it, and, being an older man, he looked and watched Paul carefully.

"You ever in the service?" he asked finally.

"Yeah," said Paul. "Navy Air."

"I can tell," said the bartender." You get to be able to tell after a while.

"I got out a year ago last July," said Paul. He wondered how the man could tell. He'd been growing his brown hair and beard out since coming home.

"My kid's in the Air Force," said the bartender.

Paul nodded.

"In Japan," the bartender told him.

"Oh," said Paul. Maybe there's a *certain look*. Maybe I have that look.

"Were you overseas?"

"Yeah, the Philippines."

"The PI. I was there in the war," said the bartender.

Paul nodded. Probably not the same PI I knew, he thought.

"I was in the Marines," the bartender told him. "I was a lot of places like that."

"I'll bet you were," said Paul.

"It's probably all changed now," said the bartender.

"Yeah." Paul lit a cigarette and shivered. It was hard to shake off the cold from outside.

"Were you on a ship?

"No, I was stationed there. Subic Bay, more or less."

"I never got up to Subic Bay during my time," said the bartender.

"There wasn't much there then," Paul told him. "Before Nam."

"You ever get to Japan?" asked the bartender.

"No," said Paul.

"Too bad. The greatest whorehouse in the world is in Japan."

"Really," said Paul.

"Sure thing. The *House of Nations*, they called it."

"Wow," said Paul. He thought it sounded familiar.

"They called it that, because you can get any kind of girl from any nation in the world there."

"Oh," said Paul. He laughed politely.

"You want another beer?" asked the bartender.

"Sure, I guess so," said Paul. He was beginning to feel better.

The bartender filled a fresh glass of Coors for Paul. "How long were you over there?" he asked.

"About two years."

"That's a long time."

"Yeah," said Paul.

"You married?"

"No, no. Not yet."

"That's a good thing. I mean, it woulda been kinda rough being away from your wife all that time."

"Yea, I guess so," said Paul.

"Steve says, that's my son, he says that all the guys that bring their wives overseas to Japan to live with them, they all end up regretting it."

"It was the same way where I was," said Paul.

"What were the women like over there?"

"I guess they were okay," said Paul.

"Just a bunch of whores, weren't they? Basically, I mean."

"I guess so," said Paul.

"Yeah, that's the trouble with some of these guys bringing these Orientals home. They been away so long they forget how good an American girl can look, and then the broad they brought home ends up going back. Happens all the damn time."

"I guess so," said Paul. "Maybe."

"I hope my son don't end up marrying one of them. Of course, I'm not saying he might not find a nice one and all that, but still...."

"Yeah," said Paul.

"A whore's a whore all her life," said the bartender.

"Yeah," said Paul, "Yeah, I guess so."

Paul paid for his beers and left, back out into the rain. It sure is cold, he thought.

CHAPTER TWO

Paul drove the Chevy through the wet streets of Santa Monica aimlessly. It would be foolish to go back to the apartment now, he thought. Or is foolish even the right word? Maybe useless is a better word. But to be honest I don't want to go back to the apartment right now, because I don't want to see Mary. Not right now. That is being honest. But it is not being *too honest*, because if I were too honest I would probably end up hurting Mary. Poor Mary. I'm not drunk, so I don't see why I'm being so fucking honest. True, I'm just being honest with myself and nobody but myself, so being honest right now can't hurt anybody. But maybe in the end it will hurt somebody. Poor Mary. I don't want to hurt Mary at all. But to be honest I am *bored* with her. Or maybe bored isn't the right word? Disinterested is a better word. I am just not interested in being with Mary anymore. Not into her blue eyes or her blond hair or her perfect softness. Why? Fuck me, I don't know why! She loves me, but I don't know why she does. I don't know why she waited two years for me and I don't know why I let her do that, but to be completely honest I really don't care why. The main thing is that I'm not in love, and I'm not going to marry her.

Paul came to a red light and stopped the car. He reached over and pushed in the cigarette lighter and then turned on the radio. The radio blared with country and western music and he turned the volume down and changed the station to KRLA. He wished that the car had an AM-FM radio, so that he could listen to the sounds of the FM stations. He lit his cigarette and the signal turned green.

Maybe, he thought, I should go down to Dago and see Don Frank? I could drive down to San Diego this weekend and see good ol' buddy Don Frank. That would be a good idea. We haven't seen each other since we got out last year. Not once since July and here it is, raining in April. Almost one whole year. I know what he's doing, he's got a silly job at a construction company and he's making lots of money. He's probably very happy making lots of money. He probably went ahead and got that new van. When was it that I called him? Was it in December or January? Does it matter when I called him? It was raining then I know. Cold and raining, just like now. He probably did get the van. He told me he'd saved up almost enough to pay cash for it and it was December or January when he said it. He's got his own apartment by now, and a new van and most likely a new surfboard.

What have I got? Bad grades in College and a shack job with a girl I don't care about anymore. Not that I don't care about how she feels. No, not that at all. And not that I give one damn or anything else about the bad grades. So? That makes for a solution, doesn't it? Chuck it all and go live off Don. What a solution! Maybe he could even get me a job with his construction company and I could be making lots of money. Live in Mission Beach with Frank and make lots of money and then take it easy next summer and surf every day. Easy. So easy. Just tell Mary I'm fed up with school, which I am obviously, because I didn't go to classes today and it's not the first time and tell her also that Don Frank has a job all lined up for me, which would be a lie. An easy lie. Sure, just lie to your girl that loves you so you can get away from her. You could even call your old buddy and arrange the lie. Easy.

Paul turned left at a signal and then turned left again and then left again and then right, so that he came back out on the street he had been on to start with and headed back in the direction he had come. He turned off the radio so he could listen to the swish of the windshield wipers and the sloshing sound of the wet street as his tires passed over it. The rah-rah voice of the announcer had bothered him vaguely. Mary would be home by now, he thought. Sweet Mary. Wondering where I am. But not worried about it. Not sweating it. Mary never sweats it. Mary is a good girl. Not a prostitute. Now why did I think that? I know why I thought it, but I don't want to think about why I thought it. There was no value in thinking it, so why did I think it? To be honest, once again it is Rosie.

Rosie is why I thought it. Rosie. Rosie. Rosie. It does not bother me to say her name.

"Rosie," he said aloud. Prostitute Rosie. It never mattered that Rosie was a prostitute when I was there, when I was with her, so why did I suddenly think that word? Maybe it did matter? Maybe it matters still? If so then I really got problems!

Either way I got problems with my head.

But I know it doesn't matter because I can indeed say her name *out loud*, Rosie, and not feel a thing. Nothing. Sure buddy. And to make matters worse, or to make them better, depending on how I try to look at it, I can also say the name Mary out loud and also not feel a thing. Except maybe boredom. Even dread. No, not that.

And Don Frank? Frank is my best old buddy from the service, from high school, from way, way back. The guy that saved my life down in Mexico, all those years ago. Maybe he can save me from this boredom now. Boredom.

That is the one thing, and it bothers me because I'm almost not worried about it.

Because to be honest I've been bored with everything since I came home. Since I got out of the Navy and came home to California and to Mary and to school and back to everything. Back to nothing.

The apartment was neat and clean when Paul got there. She had cleaned it, he thought. He could smell what smelled like chili and Mary, blonde and white and pretty and fresh, came out of the kitchen as he closed the door and smiled at him.

"I'm making chili," she said. She smiled brightly and kissed him, putting her arms around him to do so.

"It's one of any favorites," said Paul. He moved in a way that made her release him and he took off his jacket and went into the bedroom to hang it up in the closet.

Mary followed him, saying, "Well, it won't be ready for a while. It should probably simmer for a while."

"Yes," said Paul. He sat down on the bed and took off his shoes and socks. "I didn't go to school today," he said to her.

Mary stood by the door watching him. "No? Bored with it, are you? I can tell. Maybe I should, but I don't blame you."

Paul looked up at her from where he was sitting on the bed. "I don't know why I even went back to school," he said.

"I get bored with it too," said Mary. Mary was way ahead of him in her schooling, almost ready to get her degree.

"I'm very bored with it," said Paul. I had better watch it, he thought. I had better watch it or I'm going to make trouble.

"I don't blame you," she said again.

She said that differently, thought Paul. She said that differently than she did last time. And now she's wondering what's wrong.

"It sure is a dreary day anyway," said Mary.

"Yeah," said Paul. He got up and went past her into the living room and sat down on the sofa.

Mary followed him. "Do you want me to turn on the stereo?" she asked, brightly again.

"Sure. Yeah, turn it on. The radio."

"KPPR?"

"No, no. I don't care. One of the other ones."

"Okay," said Mary.

"A lousy day," said Paul.

"Yeah," said Mary. She sat down on the floor by the coffee table that was in front of him and lit a cigarette from the pack that had been lying there.

"And Easter's only a week away," she said. "Less than a week."

"I'm bored with Easter week too," said Paul. Now why, he thought, did I say that?

Mary looked at him, then looked away, taking a drag off her cigarette.

"Well, if the weather gets better, if it clears up, then you'll feel better. I don't blame you for being fed up with this weather."

"I'm not fed up," said Paul, letting it go. "I'm just bored. Bored with everything."

"The weather can do that to you," said Mary.

Why doesn't she just let it go, he thought. It's too much trouble *not to say* what I want to say, so why doesn't she just let it go?

"But," said Mary, "if the weather clears up then we could go somewhere. The river or something."

"I don't know," said Paul.

"John and Denise are going. We could go with them. Denise asked me today at school. Of course, I didn't say yes or no, I just told her..."

"I don't want to go to the river," said Paul.

"We could go somewhere else then," said Mary. "If the weather clears up."

"The idea bores me," said Paul.

"Down to San Felipe maybe," said Mary. "You want a beer, Paul?" Mary got up and went into the kitchen.

"No," he said.

"I guess I'll have one," said Mary from in the kitchen.

Paul listened to the sound of the refrigerator door opening and closing and the sound of the bottle being opened. "I don't think you should," he said.

"Why not?" she said. She came back into the living room and sat down where she had been sitting. She took a drink out of the beer and put the bottle down and lit another cigarette.

"You'll get fat," said Paul. "You're fat enough already."

Mary looked at him, brief surprise on her face. "That's not a nice thing to say," she said. She tried to smile.

"I know," agreed Paul. But it was just too much trouble not to say it, he thought.

"In fact, it wasn't very nice at all," she said. She was trying to make a joke out of it.

"But it's true," said Paul.

"Paul," she said, still trying to make it funny, "do you really think so?"

"I don't know," said Paul.

"I guess I have been getting a little too much stomach," she said.

"I haven't noticed," said Paul, feeling guilty now. It was one thing to be bored with a girl, it was another thing to insult her.

Mary pulled up her blouse exposing her stomach. She ran a hand across the smooth white flesh. "Maybe," she said. "Do you really think so, Paul?"

"No. No, you know I was just kidding."

Mary stood up and unbuttoned her blouse. She held it back and turned sideways so that Paul could look at her in profile. "Does it hang out too much?" she asked.

"Maybe it's the pants," said Paul. What does that white bra remind me of, he wondered suddenly. That *glaring* white bra.

Mary undid her pants and stepped out of them. "Now?" she asked.

"No," said Paul. "Your stomach does not hang out too much."

Mary took the blouse the rest of the way off and placed it on the coffee table. Then she stood there in front of Paul, smiling. "Let's take a shower together," she said.

"No," said Paul.

"A nice bath then. A nice hot bath."

"No," said Paul.

"Or are you bored with me too?"

Now she's angry, he thought. "Now you're angry," he said. She had every right to hate him. He was being a jerk, a total asshole.

"No," she said. "I'm not mad." She took off her bra and she came, her large breasts jiggling, and sat by him on the couch. "I just want you," she said. She put her hand down and began touching him through his pants.

"We didn't do it last night," she said. "And only once last week. We never do it anymore."

"I know," said Paul. He sat there dumbly.

"Paul, what's wrong with you? Is there something wrong with me?"

"No," he said. It's so hard not to say it now. I'm just going to have to say it and hurt her and it's too bad but there it is.

"You're not even getting hard," said Mary.

Paul stood up. "I have to leave you Mary," he said. "I'm sorry."

"There isn't much use of you going to college if it isn't what you want to do," Mrs. Sutton told her son. "Not much use at all. So, go."

"I'll find a job down there," said Paul.

"If your father was here instead of out bowling, he'd probably argue with you about moving so soon. He wants you to finish college."

"Well, I'll wait until he gets home," said Paul. "I can explain it."

"What about Mary?"

Paul said, "I don't feel like getting married."

"Well, there's nothing like getting married too young anyway," said Mrs. Sutton. "But what are you going to do? With your life I mean."

"I don't know," said Paul. "I'm not so old that I need to know. I can always finish college later. Get the GI Bill."

His mother nodded.

"Whatever I feel like doing," said Paul. For a while. Until I figure things out.

"Where are you going to live down there? You'll have to live someplace and you don't have a job waiting for you."

"With Don Frank. You remember him, right? I called him a little while ago and he's stoked that I'm coming. So, no sweat."

"What is he like these days?"

"He's still cool, Mom. You know I was overseas with him."

"You've never been the same since you came back."

Paul shrugged.

"I guess you're older now."

"Maybe," said Paul.

"You want something to eat?"

"No," said Paul. "I'm not hungry."

"You could get a job here," said his mother.

"I want to go down there, Mom. I don't know why exactly, but I just want to go."

"Then you should go," said his mother.

"I got this thing in me to go," said Paul.

"I've always told you to do the things that would make you happy."

"I know it."

"I've always told you that."

"I know it."

"If this is makes you happy."

"Partly," said Paul.

"What does that mean?"

"Well," said Paul. "I think it might make me happy. I just know that I want to move down south. I don't know why I said *partly*."

"Maybe it is only part of what you want."

"Yeah," said Paul.

"You're confused."

"Maybe. I guess maybe I am."

"Well, going down there will help that," said his mother.

"San Diego is not too far away," said Paul.

"If you go anywhere else, call us," his mother told him.

"Oh, for sure. I will for sure," said Paul.

Later in his old bed in his old room in the old house in his old neighborhood Paul lay and thought. He thought that his mother was not like the mother of any friends or person he knew. Nor was his father. I'm lucky to have them, he thought. Yes, I'm lucky. Am I too damn lucky? No, I don't think so. It's not as if I can do whatever I want. Well, I could if I wanted. I guess I would do whatever I wanted anyway. Now. If I wanted to be like that. But it isn't as if I grew up without direction, like you read about. That is what I meant. But now I could do whatever I wanted. I guess I'm a man now. Legally, anyway.

Man, or no man, he thought. I don't think we ever *grow up* to be men. No, I guess not. No, you go through life thinking the same things about stuff and getting the same reactions from similar things that you do and that have happened and will happen, and you just age as you go along. You don't just grow up one day. Now, is that true? I don't know. Where did I read or hear that? Well, it sounds true and since I thought it just now, it must be one of my rules. I read it or heard it and now it is one of my rules. One of my things. Whether it is true or not.

He lay in his bed in the room that he had slept through grade school and high school in. The room that had been the last room before the Navy. The room he had awakened in to go surfing on cold early mornings, with his friends. The room that had been his room all his life, since he could remember. He had lain awake many nights thinking and planning in this room, and now he lay awake and wondered if he was a man yet. The room seemed very small.

If I am a man now, he thought, then what will I be when I am thirty? Seven and a half years from now. Or if I am not a man now, will I be a man then? Well, to be honest I don't know about now, and I don't know about then. To be more honest I don't care. I am okay now. I am going and I am fine about it, and as far as I can see I am fine about the man thing. It doesn't matter about the man thing. Whatever. I am going to be whatever I am anyway, without thinking about it. The main thing is to be what I am, and not try to fool anybody else about it. Or to fool myself either. Mainly not to fool myself. I know...well, what do I know? OK, I don't know then.

So, he thought, I will go down there. Now after all this thinking I feel fine about going. Especially after talking with Mom. It's easy to go now. That will be great down there. With old buddy Don Frank. I hope anyway that it will be great. Well, if it isn't? So? Then I guess there will be something else. Whatever else. There is always something else, he thought, and that is something. That's good. Okay, so, I am fine about moving. I'm glad of it. Mary will also find her *something else*. Sure, she will, because there is always something else. I'm glad of that for her, and I'm glad of that for me. Good, then I am just fine about every damn thing.

Now he felt tired. He felt very tired and even sore in his muscles as if he had worked hard all that day, even though he'd done nothing, and he stretched his legs out in the cool sheets in his old bed, feeling the sore tiredness in them. It felt good to stretch and it felt good now to turn on his side and draw up his knees, and then he was asleep.

CHAPTER THREE

I t had been several years since Paul had been down to San Diego, and he found to his surprise that the freeway had been greatly improved. And the weather had cleared up since that last night at the apartment with Mary. It was a bright and sunny Saturday morning and Paul was really enjoying the drive down, despite the fact that his VW bug was causing him some trouble.

When he had come to the long rolling hills just south of Oceanside the car had not seemed to want to pull the grades. Of course, it was a 1956 model, and it had only cost him $200, which had been just about all that was left in the bank, so he decided he couldn't really complain too much.

But he felt great! He felt free. Traveling does that I suppose, he thought. He remembered that he had felt great on the plane coming back from the Philippines. That was something to remember, that flight. The flying actually. He could remember how everyone on the plane had cheered and clapped their hands when they took off from Clark AFB. That had been something. When the wheels left the ground, cheering. Everybody knew then, really knew, that they were going home. For real, going home. Back to "the world".

It only took about two hours to get to San Diego, but it took Paul another half an hour or so to find Franks' little house in Mission Beach. In the end the brand new looking green Chevy van that was parked in the street had made it easy. It was the only new van on that street, and since Paul hadn't been able to remember the street number for sure, it was lucky the van had been there.

Don Frank was asleep. And the doorbell didn't work so Paul finally gave up knocking and went around the house until he came to what he was sure was the bedroom window and rapped on it with the edge of a quarter. Franks' face had appeared suddenly in the window, the curtain lifted sideways, the familiar grin breaking out. Followed by a yawn, a motioning of the arm, and the dropping of the curtain. Paul went back around to the front door and Frank let him in, still yawning.

"Hiya Sutton," said Frank. "What time is it?"

"About noon," said Paul. Somehow, they were still using the old Navy habit of just calling each other by their surnames. It felt pretty natural.

He looked around the little, almost tiny living room into which he had been admitted. Black light posters hung from every wall and from the ceiling. The sofa was covered with an old quilt, and there were pillows, big bean bag pillows, around the three other walls of the room. Really something at night, Paul thought.

Frank was shaking his head. "Bad night last night. Bad night." He smiled and yawned again. "Well, sit down. Gotta get dressed. Shit. Man, a bad night. Sunny out huh?" He went between a curtain that hung in a doorway. "Be right out, gotta change. Gotta piss too, by god."

Paul sat down on the sofa, which sank deeply. Don Frank had not changed much, he thought. No, not much at all. Gained a little weight, maybe. There was an empty wine bottle that had once contained a half gallon of Vin Rose that had been made into a candle on the little table in front of Paul. He looked at it. For some reason which he did not understand he thought it looked ugly. Almost indecent.

Frank came back out of the bedroom and grinned at Paul. He had put on a very faded brown t-shirt and a pair of his old Navy dungarees. "Sutton," he said. "It sure is good to see you."

Paul smiled. He did not know what to say, so he smiled.

"Shit," said Frank. "It's been a long time."

"It sure has," said Paul.

They grinned at one another.

"Listen," said Frank. "You can stay here. No problem. Kinda small though, but we'll get along. Better than the PI, huh?"

"It sure is," said Paul. "Anything's better than the PI." The automatic thing to say, he thought, to anyone who had been there with you.

Frank said, "Let's go eat. Have you eaten? I'm starved."

"Sounds good," said Paul.

Frank took Paul to a small place not far from the beach that featured an 80-cent breakfast. Paul found that he was very hungry, which was probably because, he told himself, he was nervous with Frank. They did not speak while they ate, except to comment on the quality of the food, which was quite good, and Paul was grateful for the silence.

But after they had eaten, and the third cup of coffee had been poured, and they had lighted their cigarettes, Frank said, "I'm glad you came down. I'm glad you decided to move on down."

"So am I," said Paul. He knew the nervousness would go away soon, but he was impatient with it.

"Yup," said Frank. "Man, it sure was a bad night last night."

"What happened?" asked Paul.

"Oh, nothing really. Usual thing. The broads down here, well, you remember I guess about the broads down here. Remember after we got out of boot camp?"

Paul smiled at the memory. "Yes," he said.

"They haven't changed," said Frank. "No, except that there are more of them now. The hippy kind I guess you'd call it now. But it hasn't changed with them. Last night was pretty par for a Friday night."

"Hippie chicks?"

"Well, not hippie chicks. It's just the style of dress now, I guess. But girls just like those ones that we picked up on out at the East End Club. You know..."

"Rosie number two," said Paul. He smiled. And the girl Raquel, he thought.

"I don't want to hear the name," said Frank, grinning.

"Seems like such a long time ago," said Paul.

"Really. Another world."

"It's strange," said Paul.

"Yeah. And really strange to think that some of the girls here are just like the girls over there. Except they're round eyes here. Round eye hookers."

Paul smiled. He looked at the floor.

"Listen," said Frank. "I got a great idea. I got this whole next week off. Let's split somewhere. Just take off. That's why I got that van. You know I paid cash for that van."

"I know. But where? Where would we go?"

"Mexico. Or the river maybe. But Mexico. We could go really far this time, not just Baja."

"Mexico," agreed Paul. "Could we really go really far? I think I would like that. How far could we go?"

"Really far," said Frank. "Place called San Blas maybe. It's down below Mazatlán. Or just Mazatlán. More than twelve hundred miles."

"I want to go," said Paul. "I really think I want to go." He was remembering how he'd nearly drowned down there years before, and how Don Frank had somehow saved his ass.

"I know a couple of chicks that might go," said Frank.

"I don't know much south of Ensenada," said Paul. "I've never been further down than we went that one time in your old VW bus."

"You don't go that way," said Frank. "Listen, what do you think? These two girls would die to go."

"I don't know," said Paul. "I don't think I'm ready for any broads."

"It doesn't matter," said Frank. "You still have your yellow shot card?"

"Oh yeah," said Paul. "Oh yeah."

"Visas we can get in Mexico. We can get them in Nogales. We'll leave today, spend tonight in Arizona."

"Isn't Nogales in Arizona?"

"The border. But first place we come to we'll get visas. First place in Mexico."

"I don't think I want any girls to go," said Paul. He was still thinking of what he had done to Mary.

"Okay," said Frank. "No girls."

They paid for their breakfasts and left. They drove through the streets talking of the trip they would make, of the good time they would have. More than anything else Paul wanted to go. He kept thinking of how it would be and of how the trip itself, the drive and the places they would stop to eat, and the talking while they drove the van, and the driving at night, how all of it would be.

"It's tropical down there," Frank said. "Almost like the PI. It'll be hot and the water is really warm. I know where we can borrow a board for you to take. We can surf all day and drink beer all night."

Paul thought then of how it would be when they got there. There is no boredom in this, he thought. There will be a beach with nobody on it and nobody in sight, and jungle like the Philippines. It will be warm and clear and at night a lot of stars. I really don't care if any girls go. Because if any girls went...Well, what? If they went, so what? Really, what difference would it make? This trip will be good no matter if a hundred girls go. He just wasn't sure if he wanted to get to know a new girl now. Yet.

Just as they pulled up in front of the house Paul said, "Frank, if you want to take some girls or a certain girl it's fine with me. As long as they are ready to go. I mean would they be ready to go right now?"

Frank said, "It doesn't matter to me. I'll call them and see. If they're ready to leave this by this afternoon then we'll take them. If they're not, then too bad for them. They probably won't be ready. It's pretty short notice, I suppose."

They went into the house and Frank said that he would call first a friend of his to see about a surfboard. Paul sat back down on the couch. He wanted to think more about this trip. It was good to think of. He thought: It doesn't really matter about the girls going or not going. If it makes Frank happy to have the girls then it's fine. It's his van so it's his trip, more than it is mine. Anyway, maybe the girls will be good. Maybe they will be special girls, girls that would only want to go for the same reasons I want to go. But I won't think that. I'm not gonna think or hope about how the girls could be. They probably will disappoint me if I think of how they could be. Besides I've already decided it doesn't matter, and to think that way will only make it matter again. The trip itself is the important thing.

Frank hung up the phone. "I got you a board," he said happily.

"I just thought of something," said Paul. "It just hit me just now. I don't have any surf trunks." He grinned.

"I got some you can use," said Frank. "No problem."

The phone rang and Frank picked it up. Paul watched the face of his friend change. As soon as he said hello his face fell, thought Paul. Bad news.

"Yeah," said Frank sullenly into the phone. "Yeah." Pause. "A lot of warning you give me." Pause. "Sure, I do." Pause. "Alright." Short pause. "Bye." He hung up the phone.

Paul knew what it was already, before Frank said it.

"They want me to work Monday," said Frank in a low voice. "The contractor called our outfit and complained, so they want me to work all next week."

"Shit," said Paul.

"They couldn't get a hold of some of the other guys," said Frank. "I never should have answered that phone."

"It's not your fault," said Paul.

"Some of the other guys have already took off," said Frank.

"I don't have any money anyway," said Paul. "I forgot about that. I don't have any money to help with the gas and shit anyway."

"That's why I gotta work. 'Cause some of the other guys already took off I really can't get out of it. Maybe I coulda talked them out of making me work if everybody would of been around."

"I probably wouldn't even of had enough money to pay for the visa," said Paul. "No way we could have gone anyway. I got to get a job."

"Shit," said Don Frank.

"You got any stuff?" said Paul. "Let's smoke some weed."

"That's a good idea," said Frank. Then he said, "I could get you on with us for this next week. We'll be short and they'd let you work."

"I never worked in a construction company before," said Paul

"Well, it would only be temporary. You have to be in the union."

"That's okay, I'll look for another job. I gotta get a job."

"Remember," said Frank that night as they sat on the floor of the living room with the wine bottle between them, "remember that fat girl in Ding's?"

"How could I forget," said Paul. They had been drinking both wine and beer all afternoon, in addition to the three numbers they had smoked earlier, and Paul knew that he could not drink much more. Not without getting sick anyway. He knew he would have to just sip the red wine for a while, but he also knew that it was mainly his stomach that caused this. He was not drunk yet, not really. "How could I forget that one," he said. "A real pig, but she was so cool. Nancy."

"Yeah, her name was Nancy. She was really cool. She was the one that first scored weed for me."

"I didn't know that," said Paul.

"Sure, you did," said Frank. "Sure, you did. You were there."

"I don't remember it."

"That was before we knew about Carmen's or any of the other places."

"I don't remember it. I don't even remember the first time we smoked over there. I remember I was there for a month or so before we ever smoked. I don't remember ever smoking when I was in "X" division," he said.

"I don't think I did smoke in "X" division either," said Frank. "We didn't think you could get stuff over there then."

"Yeah, I remember. We were told that the weed that the Joe's tried to sell on the street was only pipe tobacco or alfalfa. But even that wasn't true. I remember once I went into the head in the Sherry Club and there were some fleetie's in there doing up a number and they shared it with me. A crazy thing to do in the head but it was actually some of the best stuff I ever had over there and those fleetie's said they bought it in the street. Did I ever tell you about that?"

"Yeah, I think I remember you telling me about that," said Frank. "It was right after you came over to Crash/Fire I think."

"Maybe so," said Paul. He still marveled that he and his best friend Don Frank had somehow been stationed at Cubi Point together. They'd lost touch for a while after high school, and each had ended up joining the Naval Air Reserve to avoid being drafted into the Army. It was a million to one.

"Remember all of the times out in back of the Sherry Club," said Frank.

"Sure. And the New Life Club too. With Eto or George or Roli. Such good times."

"It was really pretty good over there," said Frank. "We'll never have times like that again."

"No," agreed Paul, "life will never be like that again."

"An easy job with every other day off and every other day just drinking and smoking and not worrying about money or a car or anything."

"A lot of things will never be the same again," said Paul. "I remember in high school when we cared about nothing but surfing. I didn't smoke anything in those days, even cigarettes, and none of us cared about girls even. Just the waves and how cold the water would be. I could never go out surfing in the rain in sloppy waves again, in the middle of winter with the sand like ice."

"Every weekend and every day after school," said Frank. "I remember the same thing."

"But you were here in San Diego a lot," said Paul. "I was in Santa Monica and the places we went most of the time were South Bay and maybe Huntington. Beach breaks mostly. Here you got Sunset Cliffs and all the good reef breaks. I remember when I first learned about Sunset Cliffs."

"It was the same," said Frank. "I remember one day in the winter that I went out at Newbreak with this guy named Bruce. I think he ended up going to the Islands to live. But anyways it was a cold day, a big day and real overcast and scary. Then later the fog rolled in and I thought I was going to get killed out there. You couldn't see the waves coming and it was getting bigger and starting to close out and we wanted to go in but it was medium tide and we were afraid of the rocks. You couldn't see shit out there. I would never go out there on a day like that now. Just thinking of it puts a knot in my stomach."

Paul nodded. "I can see it," he said. "I can see just how it would be."

"I just surf now for fun. And these new short boards are so bitchin'! Really makes it easier and a lot more fun."

"Yeah. But some of the things these guys are doing now are impossible, really impossible. I'll never be able to catch up with some of the things guys can do now."

"I know," said Frank. "You'd have to surf every day to get anywhere nearly good, and who can afford to do that now."

"It would be nice to be rich," said Paul.

"If I was rich I'd go to Hawaii or Australia and just surf. But I still don't think I'd get anywhere near to being really good. Too old now."

"Too old and too corrupted. I'm very corrupted now. After the PI it's impossible not to be corrupted." Paul Laughed.

"True," said Frank. "We ruined our health over there. Drank too much, smoked too much, ate too many dirty tacos in Ding's, and balled too many dirty whores." He grinned. "Nothing to be done about it now." He grinned.

"I was smoking two to three packs of cigarettes over there," said Paul. "I remember sometimes, a lot of times, smoking four packs a day. Eighty cigarettes a day."

"God," said Frank. "I never did that!"

"You were always borrowing cigarettes off of me," said Paul. "So maybe I didn't really smoke that many."

"Yeah you did. I remember it."

"Join the Navy. Become corrupted," said Paul grandly. "Ship over for the PI."

"God, Sutton," said Frank, grinning.

"Some guys did," said Paul. "Some guys actually believe it or not did. They shipped over for Olongapo. For some hooker they married."

"A lot of guys got married over there," said Frank, shaking his head.

"Nobody that was in our group did," said Paul.

"No fools in our group," said Frank. "Maybe in the Port section?"

"If we were rich," said Paul, "we could go back over there and visit everybody. That would be far out. To go back as a civilian and see that town and to see how it would be as a civilian."

"I guess that would be far out," said Frank. "Really. To land in Manila and ride a Victory Liner over to Subic and look up some of those old people. And Rosie and Margaret and Eto. A lot of people. They were cool people."

"It's too bad that some big record company couldn't get interested in Eto and his band. Or in the some of the other bands."

"Someone would have to write their music for them," said Frank. "They could play really good but they couldn't write their own stuff."

"Still, it would be bitchin' to see them here in the States making it big. That was their dream, to make it big."

"And only a dream too," said Frank. "Nobody would ever go to the Philippines to find them."

"It's too bad too," said Paul.

"But it might be far out to go back," said Frank. "I wonder what Rosie would say if you walked in there some night, into the New Life Club. That would blow her mind."

"I don't think Rosie would ever blow her mind, no matter what happened. Rosie was never anything but cool and composed. Very cool mama, that Rosie."

"You say that," said Frank. "You say that, but it's not what I say. I think she was hung up on you."

"Never happen," said Paul. Unconsciously echoing the old speech patterns.

"Don't give me that Joe shit. 'Never happen'."

"Just quoting Rosie," said Paul.

"I think that was her favorite saying, you know," said Frank. "But really I think she was hung up on you. But she knew you would never stay around."

"Anyway, it doesn't matter now," Paul said.

"You two sure could fight though," said Frank. "Always fighting. And over nothing mostly. If she wasn't so hung up on you, explain why she put up with you."

"Rosie," said Paul, "was never one to be proved wrong. No matter how small..."

"And I also think," said Don Frank, "that you were hung up on her. It isn't bad for me to say it now, because it's over. The PI is over, Sutton."

Paul looked at Don Frank. He was not sure that he liked him to say that. Of course, he is right, he thought. To be honest. It shouldn't matter *NOW*. That he

FINDING ROSIE

would say I was *hung up* on her. Over there it would have mattered. But it shouldn't matter now.

"No," he said, "none of it matters now."

CHAPTER FOUR

In July Paul decided to quit his job. He decided that he certainly had enough money saved up now to do so. Nearly five thousand in the bank. Besides it was hot now. There would be nothing wrong with quitting, he thought. For a long time, he had wanted to quit anyway. He hated the job. Not the people he worked with, but the boring work itself.

He remembered his first day when Alfonso, the foreman, had introduced him to the old man he would work with. They had walked together, Paul and Alfonso, early in the morning, out into the open side yard of the high corrugated aluminum and steel three walled building where the old man worked his machine.

"Hey Roberto," Alfonso said. "I have brought you a helper."

Roberto was a tall thin old man whose body was still strong and his hair was dirty and streaked with gray. His age showed mainly in his face, which was wrinkled and pallid. It did not look to Paul as if he had ever been in the sun much in his life.

"Another new Maestro," said Roberto. "*Cabron*, you always bring me the new Maestro." He did not look at Paul while he spoke, but he grinned as if he were sharing some private joke with Alfonso. He spoke with a thick German or Polish accent, Paul could not tell which.

Alfonso said, "Listen Roberto. He is young and strong and can help you with all the big sheets. Especially with the truck beds, you can teach him, then he can drill all the holes and put in all the screws. And you can stop ruining your old back every day!"

Roberto turned to Paul. He put out a large hand with dirty brown broken fingernails. It was a large firm hand and it looked swollen to Paul. But the grip was gentle.

"My name is Robert," said the old man. "These *putas* here call me Roberto. Or just Ingles." He smiled.

"My name is Paul Sutton," said Paul, and he grinned.

"*Puto*," said Alfonso. "Even after twenty-two years you always say it wrong. Not puta, puto."

"Si, Maestro. Okay, boss. Cabron is a better word for you."

Alfonso grinned at Robert and walked away.

No, thought Paul. This Robert was not really a bad guy to work for. Except that every now and then he would get into a big rush, a big hurry, and then Paul could not work fast enough to keep up with him. Which always made him feel useless and in the way. But day after day of sweating with the very large and very heavy sheets of metal, placing them with Robert in the machine that bent them, put corrugations in them to make the sides and the backs and the doors of flat-bed trucks. And having to drill with a bit that would not stay sharp enough fifty-two or sixty or any number of holes in the diamond plate sheet that made the beds of these trucks. And then putting all the wood screws through the diamond plate and into the double 3/4" plywood sheets that lay underneath. It would take them three days to build a truck bed and then they would start on another one. Day in and day out. It was boring hot grueling work.

It's going to be okay to quit now, he thought. They can certainly find another helper apprentice for Robert. For three dollars an hour they won't have any trouble. Anyway, the hundred and five dollars a week that I brought home has made a nice pile.

He gave a proper two weeks' notice in the end. It seemed the only polite thing to do, although he would rather have quit as soon as he had thought of it, as soon as he had decided on it finally. But he felt sorry for old Robert, even though he could not think of why. Robert was certainly strong enough to get by on his own.

And Don Frank was out of work anyway, so he was glad that Paul had quit. He'd been out of work for two weeks by the time Paul came home from his last day, and he told Paul that he was going nuts by himself. "I've been going to the beach every day but I haven't been surfing that much. Just lying there and watching the girls mostly. Now we can vacation together. It's time we both had a real vacation anyway. I don't know when the Company will call back. I don't care if they ever do really. The van's paid for and the insurance is paid for a year on it."

"What about the rent?" Paul asked. He was drinking a beer like he always did when he got home from work, but this beer tasted much better than any of the others he had had in a long time. He was glad he had quit.

"What about it? It's paid up until September, and I've got plenty put away for food and gas and fun in general. Shit, we both got it made. I'm really glad you quit. We got my stereo equipment for sounds at night and we both got our boards and its summer. It's July and we got it made."

"In the old days," said Paul, "We'd have died to get this. This is one of the old dreams come true."

"We don't even have to worry about the draft," said Frank. "Or the war at all anymore. That shit's over for us, man."

"Right on! We don't have to worry about anything," said Paul, grinning.

"We'll party tonight," said Frank. "We'll get drunk and sleep it off on the beach tomorrow."

Every day it was hot and most days the waves were not too big and they were just fun waves. The water was warm enough in the mornings. And it was cool enough to cool them off during the hot afternoons. They both got tanned darkly, and every day there was a new sunburn, so that they got red and brown. They both let their hair grow much longer than they had ever been able to let it grow before and Paul washed it every night and it became streaked with sun. This reminded him of how he'd tried bleaching his dark brown hair in the eighth grade, to look more like a surfer. He laughed at the memory.

Most of all though, they surfed. Every morning they surfed, sometimes just down the block from their little house in Mission Beach or up by the PB pier, or sometimes in Ocean Beach or at one of the good reef breaks along Sunset Cliffs. And they surfed again in the evening just before the sun went down when the water would glass off again from the wind that came up in the late mornings or early afternoons. They would lie on the beach during the windy parts of the day, although it seldom got really too windy to surf. They would lie on the beach and just soak up the sun. At night, after a few beers and a lot of hot food, usually Mexican, they would sleep as if they were dead, the sun a hot memory on their skins.

Now Paul felt the old sense of real freedom coming back on him. His body felt good and his surfing had gotten back to where it had been before he went overseas in the Navy. Every day there was a sense of accomplishment that came with surfing well, and yet every day he discovered some new little thing about surfing, some new move or technique, or some new thing about the way the waves were breaking, that was a challenge for the moment or even for the next day. But he felt that the best thing about it for him was the mastery he had over what he knew already. That he could go out in the morning when the haze of clouds had not yet been burned off by the sun and the water was cool but not really too cold at all, that he could go out then and ride waves and do well and not even think of what he was doing, that was something, had to be something. He did not have to think about when to turn or when to climb for speed and even when he made a mistake he could rely on reflexes to save his ass. This he was proud of. This made him feel good about himself.

One morning they were surfing the reef break just south of the spot the locals called Garbage Hole. The morning haze was beginning to burn off, and already the sun was hot on their backs. Paul did not know the name of the spot they were surfing, but he didn't care. They had the waves to themselves, and that was important. And there was a cove-like beach below the rocky cliffs inside, so that if you lost your board you didn't have to worry about it getting smashed. It would wash up on the sand if a wave took it in too far. The waves were good and getting better. It was very glassy and there was no wind, and the tide was slowly going out. This was making the waves suck out faster over the reef and break harder and hollower. Just outside you could see clumps of seaweed lifting in the green swells.

They were sitting about three feet from each other on their boards in the water and watching the swells rolling in. One that looked to be about five foot seemed to come out of nowhere and Paul said, "Okay?"

Don Frank nodded seriously and Paul smiled his thanks. He paddled towards the beach at a slight angle, to be more in the peak when he caught it. He was looking back as he paddled, but when the wave got close to him he looked ahead, down at the nose of his board.

Now the wave had caught up to him and it was very steep where he was, sucking out from under him, the face dropping away below him. Paul felt he had it, and he stood up. He stood with his feet apart in such a way that he was comfortable, and with his weight centered on the little board. He was moving almost straight towards the beach, but more to his left than to the right. He slid quickly down the steep sucking face of the wave, and when he got to the bottom he bent low and swung into a right turn off the bottom. This carried him high back up the face of the wave and right under the lip. He sped along that way, until it got too steep, and then he dropped back down. Then the wave began to break where he was and he used the speed gained from dropping to get down around the foam. He climbed back up again from reflex and was glad he had done so. The wave passed just then over an extra shallow place in the reef and if he had not been high in the wave he would not have had enough momentum to get through. When he was safely past the spot and had pulled out of the wave he thought to himself that he should have anticipated that section. But as he turned his board around to paddle back out he was glad his reflexes had carried him through.

He was almost back outside when Frank took a wave. Paul sat on his board and watched him from behind. There was a lull now, only very small waves passed behind the one Frank had taken.

Paul watched Don Frank climbing and dropping on his wave and he could see the almost white little cove beach inside and the sandstone cliffs, and above them, much farther up, buildings that were part of California Western College. Coming down the path that was the only way down from the cliffs he could see two girls in bikinis and the little blond kid with them. He couldn't see if the kid was a boy or a girl yet. He watched them climb down and walk along the beach and stop and spread out their towels. The kid was a boy and ran towards the water. It was starting to get really hot now.

Paul could see that Don Frank was coming back out now, paddling on his knees. He turned around to check the waves and there was one almost on top of him. Surprised, he paddled hard and got into it. He passed Don Frank and did a tricky turn to show off, but his rail caught and he fell in the water.

"Was that for me or for the girls?" called Frank, laughing.

"Ah, shut up," said Paul. His board was gone, the wave had carried it away.

"I'll bet it was for the girls," said Frank, still laughing. He started up paddling back out again.

Paul had to swim all the way in to shore for his board. Once he had almost gotten to it, but another wave had picked it up again. He had to swim all the way in, and not walk the last part where it was shallow, because the bottom here was sharp with rocks and sea urchins. It was hard to swim in the knee-deep water and when he did get close to his board he felt silly looking and was tired from the strain.

But he saw what Frank had meant about the girls. It was a pretty isolated little sandy cove of a beach and both of the girls had taken off their bikini tops. One was standing with the kid by the board where it lay in the sand and pebbles by the shore. She was a small brunette and Paul could see that the kid was playing with a plastic boat. The girl had very small white breasts with erect brown nipples and she looked like she was watching the waves outside behind Paul. The other girl was laying on her back in the sun near the bottom of the cliffs. When Paul came up to where his board was the girl looked at him and smiled. She had her hands on her hips and her shoulders were back. Paul looked at her breasts openly. It had been some time since he'd seen a woman's breasts. And never outdoors.

"How's the waves?" she said, smiling like she was a friend. Or maybe wanted to be.

Paul grinned at her, picked up his board and went back out in the water to the waves.

The summer went quickly. The days were long, because of daylight saving time, but Paul often thought that they were not long enough. He was standing alone in the sand at Mission Beach and the sun was just going down. To the south he could see the long black jetties that formed the entrance of Mission Bay. Further south, just on the other side of the jetties, was Ocean Beach, and he could just see the pier and the rise of Sunset Cliffs beyond.

Not long enough for what, he asked himself. What aren't the days long enough for? Really? If the days were any longer, what good would it do? I don't know. Certainly, you couldn't surf any more than now. No, he thought, I couldn't. Wouldn't want to, anyway. Then why? Why that thought? I don't know why. Are you getting bored with this? Bored with this thing too? No! Paul sighed. He felt like he had two sides to himself. My one *self* is going to drive my other *self* crazy, he thought sarcastically. How could I ever be bored with this? This was our dream, back in High School days. Well, I won't think of it anymore. The days just aren't long enough, period. That's just that.

He lit a cigarette. The sun was almost gone now. But it was still light, and the sky was very clear. The tide was very low and the waves were small and empty. There was no wind at all, and down along the beach a girl was walking a large black dog on a leash.

Paul thought that he should go back the house now. Back to the house and the party that was starting. Back to the house and Don Frank and his party he had to have.

It was five long blocks eastward from the strand back to the little house, walking in the cool light of sundown. Paul walked slowly, passing other little houses without seeing them.

Well, it's okay that Frank has to have this party. It's really his house anyway. Small as it is, it's his. Not mine. So, it's okay. Anyway, it's not really a *party* even. Just a little get together. That's what Frank called it. A little get together. Small thing, really.

He walked along, getting closer to the house, letting the night come down and get close to him. He could feel the cool air on his face as he walked, and he could no longer feel the sun on his back.

Tomorrow, he thought, we'll probably sleep in and miss the early waves. By the time we get to the beach it'll be hot and crowded already. Well, so? So, what if we're too tired to get up early? I'm too tired now, I think.

Well, maybe. Every night is like that anyway, party or no party. But we always get up early anyway. The waves, he thought. That's what it is, that fast wet closeness. Inside and moving.

He was thinking of how it was in the water, picturing it in his mind. Little snapshots of green waves pouring over as you crouched and strained inside the hollowness, moving fast, yet not seeming to move at all. And how it was when you first went out in the morning, the water fresh and very cool until you really got wet, the tight little knot in your stomach. Dipping your arms carefully in the water, reaching deep to paddle out. Then you let a broken wave roll over you to get you really and finally wet, and used to the water, and the knot would be almost gone. Then you suddenly looked forward to getting out there, and you would paddle fast. You could see the waves breaking and you really wanted one now. You watched the waves peeling off as you paddled and automatically you would begin to head for the best place to catch them. And Don Frank would be with you and it would be hard not to grin at each other. Showing off. And paddling along next to each other and grinning with what was left of the little knot in your stomachs. If the surf was real big there would be a *big knot*, but that was something else. That was another story.

That wasn't just fun surfing, that was more serious surfing. If the surf was real big that would be fear making the knot. But on an ordinary day you would catch that first wave and just ride it, getting the feel of it back from the day before, and when you were done, the knot would be gone entirely.

Then with each wave it was unsmiling, serious, fast *fun* having. It was always like a contest too, trying to out ride whoever else was in the water. Showing off. Trying to outdo each other. Trying to outdo the waves.

No, thought Paul, it doesn't really matter about this party. It's only for tonight.

When he got back to the house he went inside and smiled at everybody.

Frank had his tape deck going and his black light on, making the room deep and colorful from the posters that hung everywhere. There was a guy and two girls there, sitting around the room on the big beanbag pillows. The guy's name was Les, and Paul had met him before. He lived in Ocean Beach and he was an old friend of Don's, but Paul didn't know the two girls.

"Here he is," said Don Frank from the sofa, "here he is. Paul, this is Jo Ann, and this is Cindy."

"Hi," said Paul, grinning. He sat down on the sofa.

"Hi," said Cindy. She was darkly tanned and she had dark hair and her teeth were very white in the soft blueness of the black light. She had a very soft, low voice.

Paul looked at her across the room. Had he seen her before?

Don Frank said, "We've been kinda waiting for you." He handed Paul a number. "Want to light it?"

"Sure," said Paul. He lit the number and dragged deeply on it twice to get it going, then he handed it to Les.

"Oh wow," said Les. He'd been listening to the music and had not been aware. He smiled and bobbed his head up and down.

Paul waited until Les had passed the number to Jo Ann, before he let the smoke out of his lungs. "That's good stuff," he said weakly.

"Les brought it," said Frank. "Where'd you say you got it, Les?"

Les looked at him, his cheeks were puffed out.

"He got it in the mail," said Cindy in her soft voice. "From a buddy in Nam." She took the number from Jo Ann.

"Maybe it's like the stuff we used to get in the PI.," said Frank. "That was pretty good stuff."

"This is good weed, real good," said Paul.

The joint was passed around again and again, until it was gone.

Paul began to relax. When the number was done he said, "Mind if I turn up the stereo a little?"

"Sure," said Don Frank. "Go ahead."

"Good idea," said Les. He was grinning happily.

"How much of that stuff did you smoke before you picked us up?" asked Jo Ann. She had a high, playful voice.

Les giggled.

"Uh oh," said Jo Ann. "He's getting the giggles."

Les giggled again.

Paul got up and went over by Les and turned up the volume on the stereo receiver from three to five. Frank had recorded the tape himself from L.P.'s, and there were several different groups on it. The music had stopped when Paul got up, and now a long electric blues number started.

"Eric Clapton," said Don Frank.

Les had stopped giggling. "Wow," he said, "listen to that guitar."

Paul went into the kitchen and got a Coors out of the refrigerator. He came back and sat down.

"You could have offered me one," said Cindy in her low deep voice.

"Oh," said Paul. He got up and went back into the kitchen.

"Me too," he heard Frank call.

Cindy came into the little kitchen. Paul opened her a beer and handed it to her. He thought she was very good looking.

"Thanks," she said. "I was only messing with you out there."

"Oh," said Paul. "That's okay." He opened another beer for Frank and walked back out of the kitchen, passing her. She followed him out and sat back down on her beanbag pillow.

Don Frank said, "Should we burn another number?"

"Sure," said Jo Ann.

"You light it this time," said Paul.

"Okay," said Frank. "Why not?"

"All this hassle over who lights it," said Cindy, but she was grinning.

"No hassle," Frank told her.

They smoked two more numbers while they listened to the music and drank beer. The music was mostly blues, but when they were done with the second number a Beatles song came on.

"What's the name of that song?" asked Les. "I can't remember the name of that song."

"The name's not important," said Cindy.

"JoJo," said Don Frank.

"It's an old song," said Jo Ann.

"Yeah, the Beatles are gone," said Les.

"Beatlemania," said Cindy. "I love the Beatles."

"Reminds you of the P.I., doesn't it?" Frank asked Paul.

"Yeah," said Paul, thinking of Santana.

"You were over there too?" asked Cindy.

"Yep," said Paul.

"Remember, Don told us that?" said Jo Ann.

"Was it cool there?" asked Cindy.

"Cool in the tropics," said Les, giggling.

"He knows what I mean," said Cindy.

"Yeah, I guess so," said Paul.

"They had some really good bands over there," said Don Frank.

"I'm going to have another beer," said Paul. He got up. "Anybody else want one?" He started for the kitchen.

"No thanks," said Les.

"Bring me one," said Don Frank.

"I'll have a coke," said Jo Ann.

"We don't have any cokes," Don Frank told her.

Paul went into the kitchen and opened the fridge. Cindy came in and stood behind him. "Do you have any wine?" she asked.

"Sure," said Paul, without looking at her. "Is Vin Rose okay?"

"Okay. Yeah, fine," she said.

"It's all we got."

"It's fine."

Paul got out two beers and set them on the sink. Then he got out the quart bottle of wine and poured her a glass. "You want any ice?"

"No, that's fine."

"Good," he said. He opened the two beers. When he turned around with them she was still standing there. "We might as well go back in," he said.

"Okay."

Paul went back in and handed Frank his beer and sat down.

"What time you wanna get up tomorrow?" he asked Frank.

"I don't know."

"What's that you're drinking?" asked Jo Ann.

"Wine," said Cindy.

"Oh. I thought it might be coke."

"No coke," said Les, and giggled.

"Never seen anybody have the giggles that long," said Don Frank.

"He hasn't really got them going yet," said Jo Ann. "Wait 'til he gets really started."

"Yeah," said Cindy. "Just wait." She giggled herself.

"Sorry we haven't got any cokes," said Don Paul. "Didn't think of it."

"Oh, she'll live," said Cindy. More giggles.

"Yeah, that's okay," said Jo Ann. "Really."

Les giggled. The music had stopped and he sounded too loud.

"Guess I better turn that tape over," said Frank. He got up and went over and turned it over.

"What time is it?" asked Paul.

"Nine-thirty," said Jo Ann, looking at her watch.

"Thanks," said Paul.

"It's not too late yet," said Cindy, looking at him.

"Yeah, it's still pretty early," said Les tightly.

The music started again. It sounded too loud now. Frank turned it down a little, and then he went back over and sat down.

"I'm getting hungry," said Jo Ann.

Les laughed. "What?" he said, giggling.

"I said I'm hungry."

"Hey, so am I," said Don Frank.

"I haven't eaten since noon," said Jo Ann.

"Let's all go get something to eat," said Frank. "Man, I'm hungry."

"It's the grass," said Cindy. "It's the munchies."

"Let's all go get a pizza," said Don Frank, standing up.

"Great idea," said Les.

"I don't think I'll go," said Paul. "You guys go ahead and go. I feel like crashing anyway."

"I'm not hungry either," said Cindy.

"Okay," said Paul.

Jo Ann had stood up already. "Well, I am," she said. "I've got the munchies for sure."

"All right, all right," said Les. He stood up. "Let's go, let's go," he said. He wasn't giggling anymore.

"You guys are coming back, aren't you?" asked Cindy.

"Sure," said Don Frank.

"So, I'll just stay here then."

"I don't know if we should leave you two alone," said Don Frank, grinning.

"It's okay," Cindy said lightly. "I trust him."

"Yeah, I'll just crash," said Paul. He stood up. "Probably be asleep when you get back."

"You don't want us to bring you anything?" asked Frank. Les and Jo Ann were already going out the door.

"No," said Paul.

"I'm just not hungry," said Cindy.

Don Frank went out the door, closing it behind him.

"He's really a cool guy," said Cindy. She was still sitting on the big beanbag chair.

"Yeah," said Paul. He grinned. He went into the kitchen and found a pack of cigarettes and lit one from the stove. He came back in and sat back down on the sofa and picked up his beer and drained it.

"If you want to go crash, that's okay by me," said Cindy. She smiled. "I'm okay by myself."

"I really am kind of tired," said Paul.

"Yeah," she said. "Have you known Don long?"

"About forever."

"How long were you guys in the Navy? I always thought the Navy was a four-year thing."

"No, just 3 years. They had active Reserve enlistments for a while. Active reserve meant going one weekend a month for a year, then two years active duty."

"You were overseas most of the time, then?"

"Yeah. Well, just 18 months." He stubbed out his cigarette.

"The only place I've ever been is Hawaii," Cindy told him.

"Did you like it?"

"I guess so. In a way."

"I like warm weather," said Paul. "The tropics. Warm and humid."

"Winter's coming," said Cindy.

"Yeah. Well, think I'll crash. Really tired."

"Oh okay, go ahead," she said. "Won't bother me. I'm kinda tired too."

"Okay. Nice meeting you," said Paul, smiling at her as he got up. He went into the bedroom, wishing there was more than just the hanging bamboo curtains for a door. He undressed down to his white shorts in the dark and got into his bed. Frank's bed was between his and the bathroom.

After a while Cindy came in through the bamboo curtain. She stood there in the dark, the weird black light from the living room behind her for a second. "Is the bathroom in here?" she asked.

"Yeah," he told her in the dark, "it's right in there."

She went into the bathroom and closed the door. The light went on and he could see it through the cracks around the edge. After a while the door opened and she stuck her head out.

"Would it be okay if I take a shower?" she asked.

"A shower?"

"I feel kind of grubby."

"Sure," he told her.

She paused, looking at him for a minute, her head black against the light from the bathroom. Then she said, "Okay."

The door was only partly closed, and he could hear the water running. He lay there on the bed in the dark, listening to the water running and the music playing in the other room. Then after a while he said, "Ah hell," and he got up, stepped out of his shorts, and went over to the bathroom door and went inside. He'd remembered that Cindy was the girl he'd seen on the beach at Sunset Cliffs with no top on.

"I can't see any way out of it," Paul told Frank one day. They had just come in from the water and the boards were safely in the back of the van that sat in the

43

parking lot at Ocean Beach. They were laying in the sand to let the sun dry them, laying on their stomachs. Paul lit a cigarette, now that his fingers were dry.

"Out of what exactly?" said Don Frank. He was watching a girl nearby.

"Well, it's almost the end of summer," said Paul.

"So?"

"So, it's going to get cold pretty soon."

"So?" said Frank. "We could go on down to San Blas for the winter."

"I don't think you'll go," said Paul.

"It wasn't my fault about the last time," said Don Frank. "That we didn't go."

"I know that. That's not what I meant."

"Well, what did you mean?"

"I just don't think you'll go."

"Sure, I'll go. It's warm down there all year 'round. Our winter is the best time down there."

"It would be a good place to go," said Paul. "And I guess maybe you'd go down to Mexico. But it would be too easy to come back. I wouldn't want to come back. Not until next summer, anyway."

"You have to come back when you run out of money," said Frank.

"How much money you got left, Frank? Exactly?"

Frank looked at him. "Why?"

"I've still got around three and a half grand left," said Paul. "I could stay a long time with that."

"I've got a little more than that left," said Frank. "But still you run out sooner or later."

"Sooner or later," agreed Paul. "But if we went to Australia you could get a job when you ran out."

"Australia?" Don Frank looked like he thought Paul must be kidding.

"Why not? There's nothing to keep me here, and in Australia there are places where it stays pretty warm all year around."

"Oh sure. And surf the rest of our lives. Sure."

"Well, you could just stay here and get married and raise kids," said Paul. "But you could do that in Australia too."

"I didn't say that," said Frank. "I didn't mean that."

"Well," said Paul, "there's nothing wrong with that. I mean, I might want to get married someday, if I ever meet some groovy enough chick. But the thing is I want to go, really just up and go you know, and not be forced by money into coming back before I was ready."

"Well, that's not what I meant."

"Well, why don't we go then?"

"It would take all of our money to get there," said Frank, exasperation in his voice.

"Yeah. I still think we ought to go," said Paul.

"We'd spend all our money getting there, and then what?"

"It doesn't cost that much to get there. You're thinking of round trip tickets or something, and I'm not. Besides, we could sell our cars too."

"Sell my van!"

"Why not? Or we could work a couple months and save up a little more cash. But I think we got enough now and I think we ought to go now."

"I'm not going to sell my van," said Don Frank, sounding very serious.

"What would you do with it, then? Put it in storage? That costs a lot of money. Or I guess you could put it in your parent's garage. They'd probably go for that, wouldn't they?"

"I don't know," said Frank. "Maybe. I guess so."

"Well, why don't we go? Let's go, Frank. I've got to go. I've just decided that it's now or never."

"Let me think it over," said Frank. "That's a big move and I've got to think it over."

CHAPTER FIVE

N ow Paul stood against the green railing of the fishing pier in Ocean Beach and thought. They had not talked of the trip again, and Paul was still waiting for Frank to make up his mind. I don't think he'll go, thought Paul. But for sure I'm going to go, alone or not.

It was a bright and sunny and hot day out on the pier. Paul stood in his white tee-shirt and his blue nylon trunks and watched the waves and the surfers below him. Frank was still out in the water and Paul could see him sitting on his board in his green trunks watching for a good wave.

He won't go because he isn't like me really, and doesn't want it, or just doesn't feel the need, Paul thought. And I can't blame him if he doesn't feel the need to go. I'm sure he would *like* to go. I want him to go. But he won't go because he knows I don't want to come back any time soon and he wants to make it like a vacation. He's honest at least. And I'm sure he won't go, so there is no use in waiting any longer.

If I'm going to have to go alone, thought Paul, I might as well hurry up and quit stalling and go.

He could see now that Frank was going to take a wave. He watched as Frank watched the wave approach him, facing the shore but turning his head back to see the wave come. As the wave reached him Frank lay prone and paddled quickly until he was in it, then stood up and turned towards the pier, going right, he climbed high in the wave for speed but the wave was moving faster than Frank was moving and it broke against his waist. Paul thought that Frank would fall, but Frank straightened out and turned in towards the beach, riding the soup, and Paul knew then that Frank was quitting and had decided to come in.

Paul walked along the pier until he came to the steps that led down into the parking lot of the beach and he went over to the van where Frank stood toweling himself and watching the waves.

"Light me a cigarette, okay?" said Don Frank when he saw that Paul had walked over. "My hands are soaked."

Paul lit two cigarettes and handed one of them to Frank. Frank held it by the filter until he had it in his mouth. "Thanks," he said.

"Getting pretty lousy out there," said Paul.

"I got disgusted," said Frank. "It might be good this afternoon when the tide goes out, though."

"Maybe," said Paul.

"I'm hungry. Let's go get something to eat."

"Okay."

They locked the boards in the van and walked up the beach to a place not too far that sold hot dogs and hamburgers and corn strips and all such things that are popular and sell well at the beach in the summer. Frank got french fries and two fried burritos and a coke in a paper cup. Paul decided that all he wanted was a coke.

They sat on the edge of one of the concrete fire pits in the sun on the beach and Frank ate while Paul talked.

"Tomorrow," said Paul, "I'm going to go to the travel agency and buy my ticket."

"You'll have to get a passport," Frank said as he chewed burrito and french fries.

"I've already got that. Last week. I picked it up last week. You can see I was prepared."

"So, you're really going to go?"

"Yeah. I have to go. I wish you'd go with me."

"I've been thinking it over," said Don Frank. He swallowed some more burrito and took a long drink of his coke. "But I don't think I want to."

"Why not?"

Frank said, "I guess I've had enough of it. I got enough of it when we were in the PI. I guess maybe I hated it over there more than I thought."

"None of us liked it at the time," said Paul. Not at first, he thought.

"I don't know. I think we *thought* we liked it. I think you liked it. But I hate it now, now that it's over with."

"Huh? I didn't know that," said Paul. "But I knew you wouldn't go."

"It's your trip," said Frank. "I think you should go. I'm all for you going. But I can't go. I don't want to go anywhere. I'd just be like extra baggage and besides it's your trip, not mine."

"I'm going to go," said Paul after a while. "I wish I could understand why I have to, though."

"You don't know why?" Don Frank grinned.

"No."

"I'll tell you why."

Paul shrugged.

"I can tell you exactly why," said Frank, looking seriously now at Paul. "You're a *romantic*. Searching for paradise in the south seas." He grinned.

"Ha Hah! Bullshit!"

"Searching for adventure and for love. I don't know why, but you're like that. I've learned that about you. You're what they call a romantic."

"Bullshit," said Paul. He wanted to change the subject.

"Well anyway, that's what I think," said Don Frank, turning his attention to his second burrito.

"A *Romantic*," said Paul sarcastically. "I don't think so. But maybe." He smiled. "Well anyway, I'm going to go."

That evening after the sun was down, when Frank came home from surfing the afternoon glass-off, he found Paul in the bedroom packing his clothes into the small plastic leather "AWOL" bag that he had carried in the service.

Frank said, "So soon? You leaving so soon? Far out. You must have got really lucky to get a ticket so soon."

Paul smiled. "Not luck. Just timing. There's a flight leaving day after tomorrow from L.A. I'll drive up to my parents tomorrow. I'll leave the Bug there. Then I'm off for Hawaii."

"Hawaii?"

"Yeah, that's the first stop," said Paul. He zipped up the bag. "Well, that's it. Not too much. I'm not taking too much. The board's a lot to have to travel with as it is."

"I know what you mean."

"In fact, if I had time to find a buyer I'd sell it. I can always get a board in Australia."

"But you might get a chance to use it on the way."

"I don't think so."

"Where will you be stopping besides Hawaii?"

"You won't believe it. You just won't believe it."

"Don't tell me," said Frank, grinning. "You gotta be kidding."

"I'm not kidding." "

"Far out," said Don Frank.

"First Hawaii. Just an hour or so there. Then Japan. An overnight in Japan, then in the morning on to Manila, with a maybe stop in Okinawa. In Manila I change planes and go on to Sidney."

"Very far out," said Frank. "How long will you have in Manila?"

"I don't know. A couple of hours or a couple of days. If I want to stay there and wait for another flight, I can. Take a layover. The ticket's good for thirty days. I have to change planes there anyway, so really I could take any flight later that's going on to Sidney."

"Well, that's far out," said Don Frank. "Listen, I gotta take a shower, then we'll go celebrate. We gotta celebrate."

"Sure," said Paul.

After Frank had showered he'd gone out to buy something to drink for the celebration. He'd told Paul he was going to get a surprise and he did. He'd brought back a bottle of Cherry Brandy and two large bottles of Seven-Up.

"I didn't expect that," said Paul. "Just like old times, huh?"

Frank was grinning happily. "Yep. Just like back in the PI." He mixed the Seven-Up and the Cherry Brandy half and half, and with lots of ice cubes.

They sat across from one another at the tiny kitchen table, with Franks' stereo playing a tape he had of Bob Dylan songs, very low.

"It's not exactly like the PI Cherry Brandy," said Paul.

"No," said Frank. "This is made from grain alcohol. The stuff over there was made from sugar cane."

"But this is good," said Paul. "This is just as good."

Sitting there like that Paul Sutton could not help but think of the old times. Sitting in Ding's or in Kong's with Frank and drinking Cherry Brandy in the morning and passing the time. It's just like Frank to do this, he thought. To get the Cherry Brandy and the Seven-Up and do this thing. To bring back the old times. Why does he do this? He has said that now that it's all over he hates it. So, I don't understand this here. Well, it doesn't matter.

Probably he does it for me. It wouldn't be nice to asked him why, so I won't. Maybe he thinks that it's not over for me. Probably he does think that, and just as probably he thinks that's okay. He thinks that it's okay for me, and probably he thinks he knows why. Should I ask him that?

"So Frank," he asked, "why did you get the Cherry Brandy? I mean, what made you think of that?"

"I don't know," Don Frank said thoughtfully. "I just thought it might be a good idea. Just came to me, I guess."

"I didn't mean it was a bad idea," Paul said quickly. "I think it was a great idea. I was just wondering how you got it. But I'm glad you did."

"It's different, anyway," said Frank, grinning again.

Maybe I'm too suspicious, thought Paul. If that's the word. I don't know if that's the right word. Anyway, it would be a lot better to think about the trip. The day after tomorrow I'll get on that plane and that will be that, no turning back, and I can't imagine *wanting* to turn back. Then why did you think of turning back, he asked himself. I don't know. Sure, you do. No, I don't think I do. I just thought that to make myself excited. Why do you need to make yourself excited? I don't know. I don't need to make myself any more excited than I am. Are you fearful now? Is that it? Are you afraid of going now, now that it's so close? I don't know. Maybe. Not fear. But you might as well be honest with yourself. Yes, I should be that. Think about the dream then. No. I don't need to think about that at all. Who knows why we have the dreams we have anyway?

"Do you ever have weird dreams?" Paul asked, thinking at the same time that he hadn't wanted to say it or to ask it and yet the words had come out anyway.

Don Frank looked at Paul. "I don't know Sutton. Sometimes I guess."

"Oh," said Paul, thinking hard. There must be some way to get out of ever having asked that.

"You know you have to wake up during your dream to ever be able to remember it," Frank said.

"Oh," said Paul.

"I read that in an article," said Frank. "I read a lot you know."

"Yes, I know you do," said Paul.

"Why?" asked Don Frank.

I knew he'd ask me that, thought Paul. Well, what the hell? I'm going away tomorrow and anyway he's an old friend, my best friend, and so what the hell? No, it won't hurt to tell him about the dream. Really the main thing is that I don't like it. Well, why don't I like it?

"Well, I had a dream like that the other night," said Paul.

"Oh yeah?" said Frank. "You must of woke up in the middle of it, if you remember it. Well, what was it? Tell me. Did you dream about orange waves or something?" Frank laughed a little and sipped his drink.

"No," said Paul, thinking that he did not really want to tell it now. "No, it wasn't anything like that."

"A sex dream then. Three chicks?"

"No, not that. Maybe you will think this means something, my dream, but I don't think it means very much. Wishful thinking, I guess."

"Something to do with the trip, I'll bet. Don't tell me the plane crashed!"

"It wasn't a nightmare," said Paul slowly. "It was a dream in color and it was the kind of dream where you see yourself. Like you would in a movie, sorta."

"Most dreams are in color," Frank said knowingly.

"It was a soft dream, it felt all soft and slow and everything in it moved very slowly. I'll tell you about it. It was a good dream while it lasted and it made me feel good, although I can't remember much that happened in it."

Then he was remembering the feeling the dream had given him while he had lain there in the dark under the covers and thought of it, just after he'd woken. He was letting that feeling come back over him now, and he hardly realized he was speaking.

"I'll tell you about it," he was saying. "It was a good dream because I felt good from it after. There was a warmth that came from what happened in the dream that I've never felt before." Paul sighed. "And all it was really, was this: I was someplace here, in the States I mean. In some big old house. I didn't recognize the house. And Rosie came in. Someone brought her in the room, I don't know who. Only I didn't think it was really Rosie at all, at first. It looked like her, but I didn't think it was because this woman did not act like Rosie. But she did look like her! And in the dream, it was as if this Rosie had just come home. It was as if she'd been gone a long time and had finally come home. Then we were hugging each other and both of us were really happy to be back together. That's what it was like, as if we were back together after some long old time that she had had to be away. Like I'd been waiting for her all this long time and she'd finally come home. And I could see both of us there hugging each other." His voice trailed off at the last words because he'd realized what he was saying.

Don Frank was grinning and nodding. But he looked serious when he said, "Sure. I'm surprised you haven't had that dream before. You know what an analyst would say don't you? Have you ever had the dream before?"

"No," said Paul.

"Well, you might have. Maybe you just don't remember it because you never woke up when you were having it before."

"I don't think so," said Paul. "I remember being surprised at the dream."

"You just weren't conscious of it before."

"I don't know why I had that dream. But I don't think it means much."

"I know why you had it. But I don't think I'd better tell you."

"Bullshit," said Paul. "You don't have to tell me your stupid idea. I know what you're thinking but it isn't true. Or if it is, it's only that it *used to be* true. I mean I don't know and can't explain the frame of mind I was in over there. But I'm not in the same frame of mind now."

"Maybe," said Frank. "Maybe you just ought to look her up when you get there. Take a couple of days and look her up. Then when you see her you'll know."

"I ought to," said Paul. "It'll probably make you rest easier."

Don Frank smiled. "Do it! Why not? Probably be fun anyway."

"If I have time," said Paul.

"Listen," said Frank. "I meant to tell you this before. Something I thought of while I was in the shower. Your board. I'll buy it."

Paul shook his head.

"Sure, why not?" said Frank. "I can sell it and get my money back. You don't need to be stuck with it traveling. There's no surf in the PI near Olongapo, remember, and you won't have time in the Islands or in Japan, so why be stuck carrying it around to hotels and stuff?"

"Alright," said Paul. "But you can just sell it and send me the coin later."

"Nah, I can give you the money now. A check, and you can cash it at the airport. Just name a reasonable price. I can take my time selling it."

"All as easy as that," said Paul. "Okay. You're a real buddy, you know that? I mean it. A real good buddy. I wish you'd go with me, but... would fifty bucks be too much?" he grinned.

"Not at all," said Frank.

After finishing the Cherry Brandy, the two young men walked down to Mission Boulevard for some tacos and beans to finish their celebration of Paul's trip.

Paul Sutton arrived at LAX at nine-fifty AM two days later. It would be just over an hour before he finally got on board the Northwest Orient plane to leave for Hawaii.

He was definitely excited now. It all felt the same. This airport, or any airport really, had always done that to him, he realized. All the people milling around, carrying bags with airline tickets on them, standing in lines, the voice of the girls announcing flights and arrivals and departures. Soon he would hear his own flight announced.

His parents had been surprised but didn't act angry or alarmed. But then he hadn't mentioned the Philippines. This was just another surfing trip. He'd be back soon. Yes, he was still thinking of going back to college, of course. Maybe the computer programming everyone was talking about nowadays. His Dad would park the VW Bug behind the garage and put a tarp over it. They'd asked him about money, but he'd told them not to worry. Yes, he would write. Of course he would.

The excitement made him thirsty and he went into the bar. The cocktail lounge it's called, he reminded himself. Man, he thought. Man, this is something. To be going overseas again and no Navy orders under your arm about when to get there or when to get back. This is something. It would be groovy to have someone to share this with, but it's good enough alone. Yes, it's certainly good enough alone. This would be something great.

He sat at a table where he could look out the big window and watch the planes. He ordered a Manhattan. The waitress asked to look at his ID, but even that didn't bother him. It was alright now to be nearly twenty-five years old and still get asked for ID.

The drink came and Paul tasted it and it tasted very good. I'm going to drink a lot of fancy drinks on this flight, he thought. They do so much for the nerves. And anyway, why not?

He watched the planes and sipped his drink and smoked a cigarette. Smoking the cigarette reminded him of the carton that Frank had suggested he buy before he got on the plane. He was grateful toward Don Frank. Frank was a great guy. Frank had always reminded him to call his parents, reminded him to send birthday and Christmas cards. Paul had always put such things off. But the main thing was that he didn't have to worry about that for a while. *They* had been what he was worried about, he realized now. Whether or not it would bother them, and what they might say or think of this trip. And it hadn't. Hadn't because Don Frank had made him stay in touch with his parents. Made him at least do the minimum things a son should do. And so, his parents, especially his Mom, still loved him.

In a way, Frank had solved another problem. Good old Don Frank, thought Paul. "Say hello to Rosie for me," was what Frank had finally said.

PART TWO

THE P I

1969-1971

CHAPTER SIX

From the sky it looked like Paul imagined Vietnam must look. It was all green and orderly looking, with the neat well-planned rice paddies divided by neat clean looking little country roads. Only there were no explosions taking place down below and he was only guessing that those were rice paddies. But as the plane dipped it's wing in a sharp bank the sun hit the shallow water and splashed its' light directly up into Paul's eyes.

The pilots' voice then came over the loudspeaker. "Uh, good afternoon, gentlemen. We are now on our final approach into Clark Air Force Base. It's fourteen thirty local time and the temperature is ninety-two degrees. For those of you who are going on to Saigon with us, we will be on the ground for about an hour." Click.

Paul sighed. It was going to be very hot out there, in this new land. Wearing his Navy blues.

The bus hadn't left Clark until four-thirty in the afternoon, so it was dark when they finally got to Naval Station Subic Bay. And it had been, as everyone who had ever made the journey agreed, the most fantastic bus ride one would ever have.

The driver was a Filipino, but it was the usual gray Navy bus. Paul had edged his way, elbowed really, in front of everybody else and had gotten the front seat by the door all to himself. So that at least some wind would hit him. But as it turned out, the front of the bus was the best place to sit anyway. The road they had taken was in the worst repair possible. It wasn't much wider than a single lane of a modern highway back home, and was filled with pot-holes, ranging in size from about a foot wide and a foot deep to three feet or more across. In many places the road was not even paved, but the dirt was hard and crusty in these places and had just as many potholes. And to make matters worse the driver, once he had gotten them safely out of Angeles City, which was the name of the town that lived off of the Air Force Base, had really opened that old bus up. Up through the cane fields, the corn fields, the rice paddies, and the jungle they had gone. The driver passing slower cars and trucks and even donkey carts, barely avoiding oncoming traffic each time. And those in the back of the bus had found it nearly impossible to keep their seats.

And all the while Paul had stared out the window, staring at the countryside, which looked even more the way he imagined Vietnam looked from down here, staring at the people who waved at the bus as they passed through the small barrios and towns, staring at the gathering darkness. And all the while wishing that he'd never come here, never in fact joined the damn Navy. Wishing that he was home.

And then when it had gotten completely dark they had come to the mountains. On the other side of these mountains was Subic Bay, the driver told them. Only half an hour more, he'd promised. The road through the mountains was in slightly better repair, so the driver took advantage of this fact by increasing his speed even more. Paul had found himself practically hypnotized by watching the road in the beams from the headlights. There were glimpses of jungle hanging out into the road, a lonely dark wooden shack here and there, and that was all there was to be seen. The road twisted and turned and rose and dropped seemingly every foot of the way. There were no street lights along the way. And then the driver had slowed, and turned on the lights inside the bus, and they had come to a gate. Paul could not imagine what kind of place he had been sent, for there was nothing to be seen but dark trees and jungle and a road. A fence disappeared into the jungle on either side of the road and there were two Marines at the gate. And a Filipino wearing some kind of a gray uniform, with a silver badge.

Then they had continued on down the road, on down the mountain they were on, until finally they began to see buildings, modern, safe looking buildings. Then there were, finally, street lights. It was two more weeks before Paul finally figured out that they had come in through the back gate of the base.

They had gone to the Naval Receiving Station in Subic and there Paul and three other guys had gotten on another bus and had taken another long ride, seven or eight miles up through the Naval Station to the NAS, Naval Air Station Cubi Point.

"The barracks are over there," the Duty sailor in Personnel had told them, pointing. "Go to barracks 19 and report to the Master at Arms. Come back here at 0800 tomorrow."

"You have any idea how long it takes to get placed in a job here?" Paul asked him.

"You'll be in "X" Division for at least four weeks, so don't worry about it. What are you striking for?"

"ABH. What's an "X" Division?" Paul felt he could not stand any more surprises.

"You'll find that out. But don't sweat it. They need guys in Crash Fire, so maybe you might get out of "X" Division early."

"Aye aye," said Paul.

"I'll bet that "X" Division is just a bunch of sweat details," one of the other new sailors said.

"I *know* it is," Paul told him.

Paul made his new rack up with the two sheets and pillow case that the Master at Arms had given him, taken off his blues and thrown them on the floor of his new locker, and then taken a long shower. There was no hot water to speak of and the Master at Arms hadn't given him a blanket. It must never get cold here, he thought. He put on clean underwear and lay down in his rack. It felt so good to close his eyes.

But then he had felt a hand shaking him and he opened his eyes only to look up at the sunlit face of his old friend Don Frank. "Jesus Christ!" said Paul. It was the morning of his first day in the Philippines.

They sat that night in the Stag Bar on base, which was the Enlisted Club close to the barracks, and talked about their immense good luck, that their first orders since "A" school back in Memphis should have brought them to the same place. Don Frank was drinking a Rum and Coke, but Paul had wanted to try his first San Miguel beer, the beer of the Philippines.

"It's not too bad," said Paul. "Kinda strong though."

"They don't use so much water making it," Don Frank told him.

"It tastes almost kind of thick."

"I guess we'll get used to that. It's the only kind of beer there is out in town."

"What's the town like? How far is it?"

"It's right outside the gate. You won't believe that town. It's crazy."

"I heard something about it. Not much. I asked this lifer in Memphis about it when I got my orders."

"Who'd you ask? Not old Chief Bigley?"

"No, I asked this first class in the Master at Arms at the barracks."

"Chief Bigley was so full of shit."

"Yeah, he was a prick." Paul lit a cigarette. "Anyway, tell me about the town. I didn't even see it when we came in."

"You wouldn't have. It's right outside the Main Gate, across a bridge. They call it *Shit River* bridge. Man, it smells like it too. And the town's all bars. Clubs, I guess."

"Lot of girls?" asked Paul.

"Yeah, guess so. Haven't seen the town at night yet, though. Only been out there once, and that was in the daytime. Lots of shops out there."

"What are the people like?"

"I dunno. I just got here two weeks ago, but I hear you gotta watch yourself out there."

"Oh?"

"I heard they'll cheat you blind Sutton. But as soon as you get your liberty card, we can go out there. I just got mine two days ago."

"I'll get one tomorrow," said Paul.

"No, you won't. You won't get one 'til next Friday at best. You gotta go to the VD lecture first, and they only give that on Thursdays."

"Wow. I'll go crazy on this base. Never could stand to stay on a base."

"Oh, I don't know. This base isn't too bad, they got everything. Different movie every other night, a bowling alley. They even got water skiing and snorkeling at the beach. Dungaree Beach."

"Are there any waves?"

"None."

"Never?"

"No. Never. We're inside a bay, remember."

"This place is going to be a bummer," said Paul.

CHAPTER SEVEN

It was a bad week. Not only was the weather very hot and very humid, but there was also so much for Paul to do. He had to check in properly. It took two days to do so, taking the check-in sheet around the base to various places to fill out the forms and get the sheet signed. The Post Office, the Chaplains' office, Operations, Education, Disbursing, Sick Bay, and a whole bunch of other places. Then there was the VD lecture, given once a week. But after the VD lecture Paul was finally given his liberty card.

"We'll go to town tonight," Frank told him that afternoon at dinner.

They sat in the chow hall at a table that was crowded with Marines that were eating like pigs.

"I don't know," said Paul.

"Ah come on. You've been here nearly a week now."

"And you've been here three weeks."

"Yeah. And I've only been in town a few times. And then only a couple of hours during the day. Besides, tomorrow night we'll both have fire watch. You're going to have watch duty every other night from now until you get out of "X" Division."

"So?" said Paul.

"So, let's go to town."

"I don't know."

"Why not?"

"I haven't been paid yet. I'm broke."

"Well, I'll buy you some beers."

"Well," said Paul.

"Come on Sutton," said Frank. "You get four pesos for every dollar. Beers are only a peso and a half. No sweat."

They went back up to the barracks to change their clothes. Nobody, thought Paul, was as cool as his friend Don Frank.

"Listen Frank," Paul said. "I got an extra five bucks that I can take."

"Save it," said Frank.

"We might lose each other out there."

"Well, it's your money. Just be careful not to flash it around." He grinned.

They caught a *Blaylocks* taxi, and the Joe drove them down to the gate. It was about seven miles down the hill and along the bays' edge to the Main Gate, and the taxi cost them 75 cents. It was 20 cents for the first mile, and five cents every half mile after that. They walked out the gate, their wallets safely in their front pockets as specified in the VD lecture, and over the crowded concrete bridge and into town. Just on the other side of the bridge they stopped and listened to the man who was speaking into the loudspeaker mike on the opposite corner from them.

"Change your dollars now, change your dollars, at Carmen's money exchange, authorized by the Central Bank of the Philippines. Change your dollars now." The man smiled a toothy Filipino smile and beckoned to them, all the while repeating his message over and over again.

Paul got twenty-one pesos for his five bucks. Four pesos and twenty centavos to one American dollar.

"It's only 3.90 to one at the bank on base," Frank told Paul.

"Yeah," said Paul, not caring much.

It was still light out, being only about five in the afternoon, but it was still warm and the town, and most of all the river over which they had just crossed, smelled like a rotting sewer.

They walked down the street, keeping close together on the crowded side-walk. Paul was amazed. The street was crowded, but not just with sailors and Marines. There were many women on the street, but not the whores and streetwalkers that he had expected from hearing the VD lecture. A lot of old ladies in clean shabby dresses and red sweaters that buttoned down the front. And young girls and boys dressed in school uniforms, very neat and very clean, and blue and white and brown. Black and brown heads bobbed everywhere. Brown scarred legs and bare feet or feet in what Paul thought of as shower shoes. Flip-flops.

And everywhere people were selling things. Suitcase like displays of cigarettes and gum set up on wooden stands with an old lady or a young girl selling their wares seemed to be everywhere. Barbecue stands that featured a small brazier of burning coals and smoking "monkey-meat" on bamboo sticks, and whole chickens. Stands that had sunglasses and belts and peace symbols and beads.

They passed doorways of shops that featured velvet paintings and carved wooden figures of bulls and *Negritos* holding spears. Shops that looked like little drug stores, their shelves crowded with things like Alka-Seltzer and Bufferin and Vibramycin.

They came to the first corner and down the street, which was filled, like every street, with an ever-moving line of Jeepneys and taxis and little motorcycles with covered side-cars, they could see cement brick and corrugated iron buildings of every size. There were two movie theaters at that first cross street, which the sign said was Rizal Avenue. One of the theaters featured English speaking movies, the other featured movies in *Tagalog*.

And everywhere the nightclubs and funky little bars. Paul could not believe this. There were more clubs than surely even the Navy could support. And still more shops jammed in here and there.

"I don't believe this place," said Paul.

"It's something else," agreed Frank.

"Look at all those *Jeepneys*," said Paul. They stopped and stood there on the curb and one of the Jeepneys pulled up and the driver grinned hugely with white teeth and motioned them to get in. They waved at him and he moved on.

"This is only the beginning of it," said Don Frank. "This is Magsaysay Blvd., and out at the end it runs into Rizal again, and Rizal runs way out of town back towards Manila."

"And there's bars all along the way, huh?"

"Clubs mostly, not just bars. And there's a live band in every one of 'em, or nearly so anyway."

"I'm not ready for this," said Paul. "You can't go bar-hopping in this town. Nobody could drink that much."

Frank laughed. "Well, there's only about a hundred really good places. That's what I heard anyway. I haven't been in any of the clubs yet."

"How're we going to know which to go to, then?" asked Paul.

"Well," said Frank, "you know that colored guy, the little one named Irving?"

"Yeah," said Paul. "I had a watch with him last night."

"Yeah, okay, he said to try the Valentine Club. It's out around the corner where Magsaysay ends, on the right-hand side he said. Said it was a big place and that it had a good band. At least he said we'd probably *think* it was a good band."

"Okay," said Paul.

"You want to ride a Jeepney out there? It's seems kinda far."

"I guess so," said Paul.

They crossed the street and hailed a Jeepney. The Jeepney was empty in the back, but there were two grinning Filipinos in the front. Paul thought they sat a little too close together, but then he'd noticed that a great many of these people were very *brotherly* to each other, even the guys. He and Frank got in the back and sat facing each other on the bench-like seats.

"The Valentine Club," said Paul.

"Shh," said Frank, giving Paul a knowing look. "Just take us for a ride Joe," he told the driver. "This ain't going to be any *special*."

"Oh no, no special," said the man driving, and he started off slowly into the crowded traffic.

The other man turned around to them and smiled, looking at Paul. Paul looked away. The Filipino said, "Hey buddy, you don't remember me? I'm from base, I work on the base." He smiled and chuckled.

"On Cubi?" Paul asked him.

"Yes, yes, at Cubi Point. You no remember me?"

All these guys look alike, thought Paul. "Maybe," he said. He looked at Frank, but Frank shook his head.

The man grinned even larger, if that was possible, and said, "Sure, sure I work in mess hall every day."

"Oh," said Paul.

"Hey, how much, uh, how much one good wallet cost?"

"Oh, I don't know," said. Paul.

"How much your wallet cost?" asked the man. "Maybe I give you money, you buy one for me, okay?"

"I bought my wallet in the states," said Paul. "I don't know how much they cost over here."

"Let me see your wallet," said the Joe. "Don't worry, I'm your friend, I no steal nothing. You take money out first." The man had a sort of hurt and at the same time innocent look on his face.

"Fuck you, Joe," said Frank with a grin.

"Hey, whatsamatta you?"

"Come on," Frank told Paul. "This is where we get out. Stop here, Joe. The driver pulled the Jeepney towards the curb and stopped. Paul and Frank got out and Frank handed the driver fifty centavos.

"One Peso," said the driver.

"Bullshit," said Frank. "But keep the change anyway." He motioned to Paul and they walked quickly away.

"It's only fifteen centavos each," Frank told Paul. "Well, here it is, the Valentine Club."

The club that they now stood in front of was big and modern looking. In the front were big glass doors with curtains behind them and an older Filipino in some kind of blue uniform standing in front. He smiled at them and held the door open for them, and they came up the steps and stepped inside.

Outside there had been a large sign proclaiming air-conditioned luxury and the coldest beer in town, but Paul was not prepared for the nearly freezing atmosphere inside. It was dark inside also, but Paul could make out the shape of many, many tables covered in white and he could see the large dance floor and the stage up front where the band would play later. On the right just inside the door was a large curving lounge type couch, and there were many girls sitting on it, all of them smiling at him and at Frank. Over in one corner sat a sailor in his whites with a girl. She giggled, and it sounded strange in that large nearly empty club.

A waiter led them to a table, a booth type thing, over against the wall. They each ordered a beer, but before the beers got there Paul and Frank were joined by a fat middle-aged woman who smiled softly at them and asked them in an even softer voice if they would like to have some company.

"I don't know," said Paul, looking at Frank. Frank shrugged.

"Very nice girls," said the lady. "I *Mama-san.* I bring you very best girls."

"Well," said Paul.

"It will be very nice," the Mama-san went on. "The girls are very nice to talk to. Nice manners. Very polite evening, only you understand that you must buy them drinks to sit with you. Not cost much."

"I don't know," said Paul. "What do you think?" he asked Frank.

Frank looked at the Mama-san. "How much are the drinks?"

"Only five pesos."

"That's too much," said Frank.

"Well, there is a cheap drink of only two-fifty. But the girls will think you are cheap-skates."

"I don't care what they think," Frank told Paul.

"I know," said Paul. He turned to the Mama-san and said, "You bring the girls and we'll work it out with them how much we'll pay for drinks."

"And bring us good looking ladies, Mama-san. Okay?" Frank smiled at her.

The Mama-san went away and the waiter brought the two San Miguel's. The bottles were coated with frost. Frank gave the waiter three Pesos, but the Joe said it would be four pesos. Beers were two Pesos in the Valentine Club, he informed them.

"This place is a clip-joint," said Frank. "That little Irving tricked us."

Paul laughed. "What's a Peso, one way or the other. Anyway, I'll buy the next round."

The girls arrived at the booth. One was tall, and the other was short. Both of them had long black hair that reached down to their waists, and both of them had light skinned flawless looking faces and arms. And they both wore simple dresses that weren't as short as one might have expected. But the tall one was extremely pretty, with her large almond shaped eyes. She smiled at Frank with her sharp white teeth glowing in the dimness of the club and sat down next to him. The girl that Paul was therefore stuck with waited until he asked her to sit down before she did so, and then her smile seemed to be merely a formality. It vanished as soon as she had sat down and she looked off across the room, seemingly concentrating on something which Paul could not see.

He looked at Frank, but Frank was not paying any attention to him. He was staring at the creature luck had brought him, asking her if she'd like a drink.

Paul cleared his throat. The girl next to him turned back around and regarded him with something very close to distaste. Then she said, suddenly, "I know you do not like me. You are a *station sailor,* and you all want something for nothing." She turned away again.

Paul did not know what to think of that. He said, "Listen honey, I'm new here. I've only been here about a week. Now, how would you like to have a drink?"

She's not too bad looking, he thought. But it was mainly the warmth of her bare brown thigh touching his, and the obvious pleasure that Frank was undergoing across the table that motivated his speech.

There was a radical change in the girl. She turned and regarded him with an open smile and said thank you. Then she asked him his name. He told her and she said her name was Betty.

"Betty," said Paul. "That's not a very Filipino sounding name."

The girl shrugged and beckoned to the waiter. The waiter came and both of the girls got five Peso drinks within a few minutes.

Don Frank smiled at Paul. The girl with him, whose name was Gina, was sitting very close to him and looking at him with something very close to adulation. Just at that moment Paul felt Betty's' hand go between his legs and he flushed. Damn, he thought. Casually he offered her a cigarette, which she managed to accept and light without removing her hand. Though Paul hardly wanted her to just now.

Frank uttered an exclamation and flushed a deep red. Paul could only laugh.

"You like me?" asked Betty into Paul's' ear a moment later.

Paul thought that surely, she must be joking. How could he possibly not like her? Or at least her hand, anyway. "Yeah," he said.

Betty removed her hand. "Maybe your friend doesn't like my friend," she said. Paul thought that surely Frank must like this Gina girl.

Frank nodded at Betty. "Oh yeah," he said. "She's very nice."

Gina said, "Then maybe you would like to take us barhopping tonight."

"Oh," said Frank.

"Sure," said Paul.

Gina explained that it would cost twenty Pesos to check the girls out of the bar and that they would have to be back at ten-thirty that night.

"That's not too bad," said Paul. "That's only ten Pesos each." It was the wrong thing to say.

"What you think?" said Betty indignantly. "You think we're cheap girls?"

"No," said Paul.

"It's twenty Pesos each," said Betty. "And that is only to check us out of the bar."

"Oh," said Paul.

"I've got to go to the head," said Frank, motioning to Paul. "We'll be right back."

Together they went into the restroom, which, unlike the rest of the club, was well lighted. But it also smelled very bad in there. Frank said hurriedly, "I'll loan you the money if you want. I know for a fact it doesn't cost much to buy a girl a drink in a club where she doesn't work. We'd end up spending just as much if we stayed here with them."

"I guess so," agreed Paul. "But are you sure you got enough money if you loan some to me?"

"How much will you need?" asked Frank.

Paul thought for a minute. He had been told by somebody, he didn't remember who, that hotel rooms only cost about ten pesos. "Thirty pesos," he told Frank.

Frank looked surprised but he loaned Paul the money. He told Paul that he had over a hundred anyway, and they went back out.

They had had to wait until nearly seven o'clock before the girls could leave, and the first thing the girls wanted was some dinner.

"Didn't you eat before? "asked Paul.

"No," Betty told him.

They went back down Magsaysay towards the gate until they came to a restaurant that was called Kong's. It turned out to be fairly inexpensive and everyone ate, Paul and Frank ignoring the advice given to them in the famous VD lectures about avoiding food in town.

Then they went to a nearby club that was named the Sierra Club, and they went into the downstairs portion and ordered drinks and danced to the music. After a while a girl, a beautiful little girl with very long soft looking hair named *Baby Lopez*, came out and sang. She sounded just exactly like Aretha Franklin, and she sang Aretha Franklin songs. Betty and Gina seemed to enjoy this very much.

Later they went to another club called the Rocket Room where they featured another girl, and this one was a Filipina Janis Joplin. She was very, very good. Betty and Gina had never heard of J.J. But it seemed to Paul that as long as the performers got a lot of applause, both Betty and Gina enjoyed it just as much as he and Don.

Everywhere they went Betty managed to give Paul a little squeeze where it counted. So, when Frank announced it was after ten-thirty, Paul asked Betty where there might be a good hotel. The curfew was midnight in town.

The four of them went a little time after that to the Newport Hotel. The rooms came to twelve pesos each, and by this time that left Paul with only 19 pesos.

The room was spare, containing only a large bed with only a sheet, a small dresser type table with a mirror, and a sink in the corner. But there were clean towels folded on the bed and a large fan overhead, which the "bellboy", if that was what he could be called, turned on for them with a smile. He asked Paul if he would like a beer, and Paul said no, and the boy left. Paul did not tip him.

Betty sat on the bed, so Paul, feeling rather silly, lit a cigarette.

"This is only *short-time*," Betty said. "No overnight."

"Okay," said Paul. He took off his shirt and sat down on the end of the bed and took off his shoes.

"How much you give me," asked Betty. She stood up and unzipped her dress, letting it fall to the floor. Paul saw that she had much belly, and that it was covered with stretch marks.

"I don't know," he said. "I only got 19 pesos."

"Only 19 pesos!" she exclaimed. "What you think of me?"

Paul stood up and took off his pants and then his underwear. He noticed an odd look come into her eyes.

"Only 19 pesos," she said dully, and she looked away.

"It's all I got," said Paul. "Take it or leave it."

She took it.

Three days later Paul woke up to take a piss with the most exquisite pain he had ever had to endure. Don Frank was lucky and did not have to go to sickbay along with Paul. They had asked him the name of the girl and what club she worked in and then they gave him two of the most painful but wonderful shots he had ever had. Plus, two weeks restriction to the base.

Paul did not mind, and he swore he would avoid such temptation in the future. He also decided never to visit the Valentine Club again, a proposition Frank readily agreed to.

CHAPTER EIGHT

At exactly seven twenty-five that morning Paul pushed down the button on the radio mike at the desk he was sitting at and said, "Cubi zero-zero, attention all stations, this is Cubi one with morning radio check. All stations stand by to acknowledge when called." He paused and then said, "Cubi two." He released the mike button.

"Cubi two, loud and clear," came the reply from the Crash Captains' truck.

"Cubi three," said Paul in a steady clear voice.

"Cubi three, loud and clear."

Paul continued calling the stations listed on the sheet of paper that lay under the glass top of the desk until, finally, he got to the tower, the last one on the list. "Cubi tower, time and radio check," said Paul.

"This is Cubi tower," came the laconic voice, "loud and clear. Time: zero seven two seven."

"Roger tower," said Paul. "Cubi zero-zero, this is Cubi one, secure from morning radio check." Paul then picked up the yellow mike of the crash house intercom and told everybody to fall in for morning quarters in the barn outside. Frank passed through the office on his way from the bunk room out to the barn, where the fire trucks were kept. He waved and grinned at Paul.

Paul sat back in his chair and lit a cigarette. This was the best time of the day on a work day, he thought. Your duty section was relieved and you get to start two days off in about three minutes. Just as soon as they got through with quarters outside, somebody from the other section will come in here to relieve me. Paul smiled. It was a Saturday morning and he wouldn't have to come back here until Monday morning. Of course, I've been here since Thursday morning, he thought. But today was going to be a really groovy day. Surfing. Imagine that.

Little Ed came into the office. He grinned at Paul, but the grin didn't last long. "I relieve you," he told Paul.

"You got the morning desk watch, huh?" said Paul.

"I got the *all-day* desk watch," said Little Ed. "The sonofabitch watch."

"That's a bummer," agreed Paul. He signed the logbook, placing Ed's name as his relief.

"Glenn is late to work this morning," said Ed. "Again. He is very *drifty*."

"I've heard that," said Paul, laughing. He grinned at Little Ed and stood up from the desk. "Well, today is the day."

"What day? I don't want to hear about all the fun you're going to have today."

"Don Frank and I are going up to San Miguel today," said Paul.

"I hope there's no waves," said Ed, grinning.

"You're the ones that told me about it. You and Drifty."

"Well, we went twice. The first time there was waves. The second time there weren't any. But I hope you guys are lucky. Let me know what happens."

Paul told him that he would and left the office. He thought Little Ed and Glenn were cool dudes, both being from California, like himself and Don Frank. They never got to hang out with them anymore, not since being assigned to opposite duty sections here in Crash/Fire six months before. But they had hung out with them some back when they were all still in X-division. They had all taken to hanging out at the New Life Club out in town, where the bands specialized in music by Cream and Santana and other bands popular back home. Paul thought it was kind of a bummer that Little Ed and Glenn "Drifty" Drake couldn't be in the Starboard duty section with him and Don Frank, but that was the Navy for you.

He was barely in time to catch the nickel-snatcher up the hill to the barracks.

Frank and Paul had a big breakfast in the chow hall, then went upstairs in the barracks to the third deck, the other home of the crash/fire crew, the air terminal, and runway support personnel. They took showers, put their trunks on underneath their pants, and went downstairs and got a cab down the hill to the main gate and town. They took their swim fins and beach towels with them. Nobody had a surfboard here. They would have to settle for bodysurfing. If there were any waves.

On the way down the hill Frank said to Paul, "Do you think there'll be any surf?"

"I don't know," said Paul. "I sure hope so."

"So, do I. We've been here nearly four months now and haven't seen wave one."

"Yeah, but plenty of good skin-diving," said Paul sarcastically.

"Oh sure. Dungaree Beach. Grande Island. Nice warm water, nice and clear. Weird blue fish and water snakes. Shit on that. I want some waves."

"That's what we get for being from California," said Paul.

They got another cab just on the other side of the bridge in town and told the driver to take them to the Victory Liner Station. This part of it, the necessary long ride on the Victory Liner bus, was the part that Paul did not like. He thought that probably Frank did not like it either, but he didn't ask him. And he was sure Frank would say nothing. Being well inside the shelter of Subic Bay meant that no swells ever came in to form and break as waves on any nearby beach. San Miguel Communications Station, where they were headed, faced more openly towards the South China Sea. It was rumored to often catch some swell and had a nice long sandy beach. Both Paul and Don Frank felt it was probably worth a try. Paul wasn't sure he believed any of Little Ed's stories though.

They got seats in the back of the big red and white Victory Liner bus and sat waiting for it to fill up. Many different types of people got on the bus. Paul could see from the way they were dressed which ones were farmers and which were city people. There were even some rather well dressed young people that Paul thought must be college students. But nobody got on the bus carrying any chickens in boxes or anything like that. I have heard, he told himself, a few too many stories about the Victory Liners.

Then off they went, north out along the long winding road that hugged the shore of Subic Bay until it was just past White Rock Beach, and then turned in through the hills and through a large well cultivated valley, green and lush, passing through little towns and barrios, until they came close to the west coast of Luzon. The South China Sea was just on the other side of the mountains. Off the road were many things to see, old men and their donkeys, men and women working the fields. Caribou grazing as lazily as any cow back in *the world*. But Paul did not really see these things. He thought only of the waves that might, hopefully, be waiting for him and Don Frank.

Frank was taking pictures out through the window with his Minolta camera.

The road ran all the way up into the Lingayen Gulf, but Paul and Frank got off the bus long before that. They got off the bus at the little town that stood outside the gate of the Naval Communications Station at San Miguel. There was nobody standing around near them, so they shared a big fat doobie before they went in the gate.

And they had some small trouble getting in through the gate. The Marine sentry told them never to walk through the gate again, but instead to ride through in a jeepney or cab. The lecture made both of them sweaty and nervous, but it really didn't last more than a minute. Then they caught an on-base Jeepney and went down to the beach. Paul thought it was fantastic.

The beach was wide and it consisted of bright white sand, the grains so large that Paul and Frank joked that it was the next best thing to gravel. A fence ran along the beach just behind the sand in both directions until it went out of sight in the distance. It was a long beach. Paul thought of Huntington Beach back home. But it had ugly brown dirty sand compared to this.

From where they stood they could not see any waves yet. The sand of the beach on the other side of the wire fence made a hill, which was too high to allow them to see the shore. But they thought they could hear the sound of surf breaking. They looked at each other, smiles breaking out on their faces, and then they had to laugh. Then they ran laughing across the little road and through the open gate in the fence and across the hot white sand until they came to the top of the rise. They stopped and looked out on the waves and the sea.

"My God Frank! It's gotta be eight feet," said Paul, awe in his voice. "I swear to God it's eight feet high. Goddamn."

"Man," was all Frank managed. He knelt down in the sand on one knee and began snapping pictures.

The water was very blue. It sparkled in the sun. There was not a cloud in the sky. There was only a very slight off-shore breeze blowing. It was a warm breeze.

The surf rolled in long lines that approached the shore at a slight angle from the west, coming in nearly straight on towards the beach. But the swells would peak and begin to break from that peak and peel off nearly perfectly in both directions. Paul guessed that the tide was medium, midway between high and low. He also guessed that the tide was slowly going out. "I wish I had a board," he told Frank. "I wish more than anything I had a board." He began to take off his outer clothes, and Frank did the same, having exhausted his roll of film.

The water was only slightly cooler than it was back in Subic Bay. The water, Paul guessed., is being stirred up by the waves, bringing the colder water up from the bottom. He thought the water temperature was probably around 75 degrees. It felt good on his skin. And the bottom was all sand. That made him very happy.

They put their fins on in the water and swam, diving under the broken waves, out to where the waves were just beginning to break.

Paul yelled to Frank, "It's closer to ten feet."

"I know. It's bitchin'."

Paul took off late on a large swell and went left. He wished almost immediately that he had at least a belly board, because the wave was very fast. But he was not afraid. The warm water made you feel confident and secure. He didn't make the wave, or any others that day, but the speed and the feeling of freedom and the salt taste in his mouth and the tiredness that came from all the swimming made him forget all about the Navy.

Late in the afternoon they caught the Liberty Bus from San Miguel back to Subic, and they laughed at their shared fantasy of surfing. The waves had barely been a foot or two high in reality, and each of them had only managed to catch a little push towards the shore, just enough, for a few seconds, to remind them of how surfing felt. They laughed at all this and remembered the good times back home in "*the world*". They had learned there was no hope of surfing here in the PI, at least not on this part of the island.

Later they stopped in town and ate fried rice and hot canned chili con carne and then they went into Ding's club and drank Cherry Brandy until it was time to go back to the base before curfew. They talked of all the waves they had ridden back home at certain breaks and of how they must go down to Mexico when they got home, because it was so worth it. It had been a beautiful day.

CHAPTER NINE

He woke up more or less all at once, realizing a moment later that he'd been tossing and turning about an hour while his body tried to decide whether it was time to get up yet. It was completely dark in the room, but he could hear the Joe's working in the hall and in the other rooms. He threw the sheet off and got out of bed, groping his way to the light switch and turned on the light. He knew where he was. He was in town in Sam's Hotel.

It was ten in the morning and it was Friday and it was his day off and it was already hot as shit spiked with horseradish. He stood in front of the hotel and rubbed his face with his hands. Not that it mattered what day of the week it was. Not in Olongapo. The only things that mattered was that he didn't have to play Navy today and that he still had plenty of money left from the day before. He reflected sadly that it wouldn't be until a week from Saturday that he had another two days off. But to hell with it. He turned and walked. The sky was blue and warm and the air was still and warm and the street was dirty and the town still smelled. You never got used to the smell. On the other hand, he thought, he still couldn't *identify* the smell. He went into Ding's Beer Garden. It would be cool and quiet in there and he would have a beer.

It was cool but it wasn't quiet. The band was already there practicing. Then he saw Frank, sitting over by the juke box with a beer in his hand and waving at him with the other. He grinned and went over, giving the waiter the sign for a beer.

"Morning Frank," he said.

"Shit," said Don Frank. But he smiled.

"I've still got nearly forty pesos left. I'm guess I'm going to get drunk today."

"What! You mean you got a free *overnight* last night? Wow Sutton, I didn't know you did those things."

"I didn't do an overnight last night," said Paul.

"I thought you paid for a room at Sam's yesterday afternoon."

"I did. And I slept in it. Alone." Paul had never gotten over the embarrassment of catching the clap on his first Liberty in town. He still hadn't gone back to the Valentine Club. What was her name again? Betty. He grimaced at the memory.

"Oh. Well..."

"Well what?" asked Paul. "You stay at Linda's last night?"

"Yep." Frank gave Paul that satisfied look, then he said, "Here's your beer."

Paul looked up to see Nick, his number two favorite waiter, bringing him his San Miguel. Nick was all smiles this morning. "Took long enough Joe," said Paul.

"Had to find cold one," said Nick, his smile replaced by a look of injured pride.

"Okay," said Paul and gave him two Pesos. He always tipped Nick.

Nick turned to Frank and held up one brown finger.

"No, not yet," said Frank.

The Filipino went away. "Fucking Joe's," said Don Frank evenly.

Paul drank about three long swallows of his beer and put the bottle down on the table. The beer wasn't cold yet, only cool. He reflected that the ice probably hadn't been delivered yet. He lit a cigarette, noticing that his pack was almost empty. He would have to go on base later today and buy a couple of packs. He never bought cigs out in town. He asked Frank what he was going to do today.

"I don't know. We could get a bottle of Cherry Brandy and get drunk."

"I suddenly don't feel like getting drunk" said Paul.

"Neither do I really. But there's never nothing else to do."

They sat in silence for a minute, listening to the band practice one part of a song over and over again. Paul felt impatience welling up in him again. Suddenly he said, "You got any money?"

"Yeah. Why?"

"Let's go over to Kong's and eat."

"Okay."

Kong's Restaurant was right across the street from Ding's and it was air conditioned. It wasn't crowded yet though, most of the Hostess women were probably still in bed. Paul and Frank found a table back in a corner and they both ordered fried rice, chili beans, and cokes. The cokes because they were *safe*, the chili because it was not only good but came out of a can and was therefore *safe*, and the fried rice because it tasted good and had never made them sick yet.

Paul lit a cigarette after the cokes came and sighed. He was beginning to feel lousy again. He didn't like that. But there wasn't much to do about it. He felt lousy because there was nothing to do. Nothing that he hadn't done a hundred times already. He wished he had something. Like his friend Little Ed. Every night Ed went into the New Life Club and just sat and listened to the bands that played there. Paul liked the music there too. It was good. They had two bands there and they took turns playing and they both played really well. But he just couldn't get as jazzed on it as Ed was. It got boring after a while. Maybe because Paul didn't dance. And Don Frank? Paul looked at Frank. The sonofabitch just looked too damned satisfied.

"How're you and Linda getting along?" he asked him.

"Okay," said Frank. "She tried to give me some shit last night about how she had a customer who was gonna give her a hundred pesos and how she gave it all up for me."

"She just wants you to give her some money once in a while," said Paul.

"I know it. But she makes enough while I'm on duty."

"You sure of that?"

"She's alive, isn't she?"

After they had eaten Paul and Frank had gone back on the base. Paul wanted to get some cigarettes.

"You got some in your locker, don't ya?" asked Frank.

"Yeah, but I don't feel like going all the way up the hill."

"Well, I want to go buy some film while they still got some in stock. The America is pulling in tomorrow. But I need to get my camera out of my locker."

"You shittin' me? About the ship?"

"No."

"How long they going to be in?"

"I don't know. Listen, I'll pay for the taxi. We can hitch-hike back down."

"Nah. I really don't feel like going up there right now. I'll get my cigarettes down here and meet you in Ding's later on."

So, Frank had gone on back up the hill and Paul had gone back out in town alone after visiting the Exchange, where he got two packs of smokes. It didn't bother him to be alone out in town. After twelve months there was nothing to be afraid of. Besides, it gave him a chance to think.

He walked aimlessly out Magsaysay Ave. towards Rizal, wondering where he should go. He stopped and bought a pack of JuicyFruit gum from an aged woman who sold such things out of a suitcase contraption on the street. He didn't feel like going back into Kong's or over to Ding's yet. Then he had a thought. What he wanted was a good cold mixed drink. A real cocktail. A good rum and coke or something like that. But he wouldn't be able to get one around here. In Kong's maybe, but there were too many girls in there, and he was afraid he might run into one he knew. He knew where he would go. Way out Rizal, to the big square, the more or less business section of the town. Papagayos' Restaurant supposedly had good drinks. They had the best Mexican food in town so they should have good drinks too. Paul hailed a Jeepney and jumped in next to the driver.

"Hey buddy, where you go?" asked the driver after a while, smiling at Paul with his rotten teeth.

"This ain't no damn Special," Paul said matter-of-factly. There was an old lady and some kids in school clothes in the back.

"No, no. I know, no Special." The driver smiled even bigger. "Maybe you go see your girl now huh? Bang, bang?" The driver laughed.

"No girl either," said Paul.

"Oh, maybe you like Benny Boy?" The driver laughed again at his own joke.

"Shut the fuck up Joe." Paul had been through this conversation many times, and he knew his part well by now.

"I just joke, only," said the driver still smiling, and he reached over and patted Paul on the shoulder.

When they got to the traffic circle where the big square was Paul got out and gave the driver his fifteen centavos and crossed the street. Here there were people selling everything. Fresh fruits and vegetables, cigarettes at black market prices, illegal money changers standing around with great wads of bills in their hands, smoked fish, dried fish, cured squid, hot corn on the cob and hot rice. There were beauty shops that catered to the hookers and dress shops and leather shops and many of the little markets that sold everything, called Sari-Sari Stores. On the opposite corner from where Paul stood in the crowd of moving brown was Papagayos Restaurant. He crossed the street and went inside.

It was quite cool inside and sort of dim and Paul sat down at a table and ordered a whiskey sour. The place was empty except for him and an older American couple across the room. An officer and his wife Paul guessed. The drink came and it was good but it cost six pesos. Or one American dollar, as the waiter was so kind to inform. The exchange rate had gone up. Paul decided to have just this one drink and then go back to Ding's. Maybe he'd walk back, and then Frank would be back by then. But it was so damned hot outside. He lit a cigarette and decided to nurse his drink for at least an hour.

He didn't actually see her come in. But he heard the door open and close, so naturally he'd turned around. Just out of idle curiosity, as he told himself much later.

For one thing she was pretty tall. Maybe at least five seven, and he was only five eight, standing up as straight as he could. Filipinas aren't known for their great stature. And she wasn't skinny or fat either. Not slightly thin, nor on the "heavy side". She was, at first glance, just perfect, thought Paul. She had on the shortest skirt he had ever seen a Filipina wear during daylight hours, and her legs were bare, dark, hairless, and looked to be perfectly muscled and well-shaped. Yes, and her skin was dark brown, dark even for her race. Her hair was very long, midnight black and thick and shiny, and it hung with only a slight wave all the way down past the middle of her back.

But her face! She saw him watching her and smiled at him. He turned back around to his drink as casually as he could, feeling her eyes on him. The man and his wife were staring across at him. He looked down into his drink. Her teeth had been very white. When he turned around again she was gone. She was the prettiest woman he'd ever seen.

CHAPTER 10

A t three in the afternoon Paul was still sitting alone at Ding's waiting for Don Frank. He was on his fourth beer and was beginning to feel them. He felt a little tired also. The whiskey sour had long since worn off.

He thought that Frank had probably forgotten about him and gone off to Dungaree Beach to go water skiing with Bob or something. Or else he'd gone back over to Linda's like he always did. To relieve his frustrations.

If I had a girlfriend in this town, he thought, then probably I would be doing that too. Not that I really want a *girlfriend*. But it would be better than a hand-job in the Jolo Club. Yeah, but so what?

Just then Linda walked in through the door letting the bright light of the afternoon shine briefly behind her. She was short and maybe a bit stocky and Frank said that her best feature was her personality, other than her bedtime talents anyway. She saw Paul and came over to the table and dropped her purse on it. She sat down across the table from him. She was not smiling her usual smile and she did not say anything.

Paul said, "Have you seen Frank?"

She shrugged.

"He's supposed to meet me here," said Paul.

She shrugged again and began looking for something in her purse.

"He's three hours late," said Paul.

"He was at my house," she said now. She lit a Salem and said, "But he left."

"Well, where was he going?"

She made a bored look. "I don't know. I did not ask him. Why should I care where he goes?"

Paul sighed. "You had another fight," he stated.

"He is no good," said Linda.

"You guys sure fight a lot."

"He is no good. He never gives me any money. He has no respect for me."

"Sure he does," said Paul.

"If he respected me, he would give me some money. Because he's a *station sailor* he thinks he can do what he wants. Station sailor boyfriend no good."

"True," said Paul. He knew the working girls made their money, their *real money*, from the sailors and Marines that visited Olongapo as a Liberty Call, off their ships. The war in Viet Nam gave those men bigger paychecks, with combat pay and hazardous duty pay and such, often tax free too.

"I don't want him to come see me anymore," Linda told him, and looked down at the table.

"Listen," said Paul, "Don's got some pride too. All these guys on the base are always bragging about their girlfriends and how much the girls do for them and how they don't ever give the girls *any* money."

"Bullshit. *Tacamona*. I do much for him. He knows. And I know he's not rich. But he is always going barhopping and buying other girls drinks. He is big *butterfly*. I know that's why he is always so broke."

Paul said slowly, "About the only place he ever goes from here is across the street to the New Life Club. There isn't a girl in there worth buying gum for. And the music there is about the best in the PI."

"So?" She was making the bored look again.

"So you think he should sit in here all night and watch you with a customer and *pretend* to have a good time?"

"I have to work. He knows that, and you know that."

"That's not what I mean. You know that isn't what I mean. But Don doesn't spend money on those other girls." Not all the time anyway, he thought.

"Maybe yes, maybe no. I have girlfriends in many clubs," said Linda.

It is the same with all these girls, thought Paul. You just couldn't get the idea through to them, not at all. "Listen," he said, thinking he would give it one more try. "Do you or don't you like Don?"

"Like? What you mean, *like*? Either he is good to me or not. If he is good to me, then I will be good to him. He knows that."

"I mean, how you feel about him. Like, do you *love* him? Do you feel happy when you see him? You know...?"

"Maybe. I don't know." She shrugged.

Paul drained the last of his beer. They are all the same, he thought.

"Well," he said, "I gotta go. I'm tired of waiting for the jerk. If he comes in tell him I went to Kong's and I'll be at the Sherry Club tonight." He started to walk away from the table.

"If you see him tell him I don't want him to come to see me anymore."

"Sure," said Paul, and he walked out into the heavy afternoon heat.

The street was crowded on both sides with all the afternoon street vendors, girls going to work, sailors in their whites just out on liberty from their ships, and sailors like him, in civvies, "station" sailors. The street was filled with the slow moving traffic of Jeepneys, taxis, motorcycles, bikes, and occasionally, a shore patrol truck. Paul stood on the curb in front of Ding's and wondered what to do. Kong's would be crowded. Over-crowded. He didn't want to go in there. He couldn't think of any place he really wanted to go. So, he decided to go over to the New Life Club and see if there was anyone there. He crossed the street, holding up traffic.

Don Frank was there, drinking a coke and talking to Eto. Eto was the lead guitar player in one of the bands that played there, the Blues Highway. It was a good band. And Eto was one of the best electric blues guitar players that Paul had ever heard live. Paul shook hands with him in the manner that was in use and sat down.

"Where the hell were you?" he said to Frank.

"Over at Linda's. I went over to Ding's but you weren't there."

"What time did you go over there?"

"About eleven thirty or twelve. I don't know. I told Nick where you could find me."

"Nick didn't say a word to me. Fucking Joe. Sorry Eto, but you know how it is."

Eto laughed. "Sure man." Eto was short and skinny and he had the most expressive face for a Filipino that Paul had seen yet. When he smiled all his upper gums showed along with his large, well-spaced white teeth. Paul liked him.

"You guys going to play tonight?" he asked.

"Sure, if everybody shows up. At five."

"Play some blues for me, will you?"

"Sure, sure." Eto laughed softly.

"We were just going to go do some numbers," said Frank.

"Out back?" asked Paul.

"Yeah," said Eto.

"Let me get a coke first," said Paul. He felt better already. "You want a coke or a beer or anything Eto?"

"Sure, a beer," said Eto, grinning widely. "Thank you."

Paul went up to the bar and got a beer and a cold coke and then they went out back and sat in the shade under a green wooden awning on wooden coke crates and smoked up a few numbers.

By five that afternoon they were all pretty much wasted, and since the other four guys in the band had shown up Eto went up on the little stage that was crammed with amps and speakers and two sets of double Ludwigs and they warmed up and began to play an old Eric Clapton/John Mayall tune and Eto played it very well. That first number lasted half an hour, and Paul and Frank sat at the table right in front of the stage and drifted.

CHAPTER 11

A t six o'clock the other band, the Black Hawks, a sort of soul music group, came on and Frank and Paul left and walked down to Kong's to get some more fried rice in their stomachs. Paul felt mellow and said so to Frank.

"Mellow's the word," said Don Frank, a big grin on his face. "They call me mellow yellow," he sang.

They talked as they ate.

"I guess you and Linda had another fight," said Paul

"Yeah. How'd you know? I just went over to her house and she wouldn't talk to me. Just like that. But she was fine when I left her this morning."

"Yeah. Well, these broads are all the same." Paul was just saying what he'd heard. He didn't have a girlfriend in town. There was just Mary back home.

"I know it. I don't give a damn."

"Sure. Neither does she apparently. I saw her in Ding's and we talked for a while. Just before I walked over here. She told me to tell you she didn't want you to come to see her anymore, but shit..."

"I know it."

"I think she's hung up on you," said Paul. "Otherwise she wouldn't have put up with you this long."

"None of these broads in this town ever get hung up on anyone. Not really. They don't know what love is. They don't even know what sex is. Not really."

"Maybe," said Paul. "But what you going to do about Linda?"

"I'll go over and talk to her when I get through eating I guess. See what happens."

"She thinks you been messing around with other girls too much. Spending money on them instead of her. I told her that that was a bunch of crap. But you know what she said to that."

"What?"

"Oh, you know. Says she's got spies all over town and all that crap. Typical."

"Yeah. Well, I'll go over and talk to her and see what happens."

"Okay," said Paul. "I'll meet you over at the Sherry Club. I haven't been in there in a while."

"Sherry Club, yeah. It's almost six-thirty now. I'll be there by seven or so. Wait for me there, don't split somewhere."

Paul laughed. "Okay," he said.

Don Frank left the money he owed on the table and got up and went out the door. Paul smiled. You couldn't tell for sure, he thought, but it almost seemed as if Frank was getting heavy on that girl. A hooker.

Paul walked into the Sherry Club and sat down at a table in back along the wall. He could see that the club was beginning to fill up, but he knew it wouldn't really seem crowded until after seven, when most of the girls who worked there arrived. Some of them were here already. He considered many of them ugly. And he wondered again why this club, which was always so crowded because of the quality of the music, why it didn't have any good looking girls. Ding's had at least four popular girls, but he couldn't imagine anyone sitting in Ding's all night to listen to their music. It wasn't that bad, but the band in Ding's didn't have any *interpretation*. They just imitated. Here both bands gave the music they played their soul, he thought. Or maybe it was because they were all pot-heads. Paul didn't know what it was, but both the bands here and the two bands over in the New Life Club could make you think or feel or even believe the music, believe it meant something to them. Even though they played the music of established English and American groups.

Eto walked by the table, having just arrived from wherever he'd been, and waved at Paul. Paul knew it was getting close to seven, and time for the Blues Highway's first set of the night.

At seven the Black Hawks finished their last number of the hour-long set, Soul Sacrifice by Santana, introduced Eto's group the Blues Highway, and began leaving the instrument packed stage. Paul ordered a beer and wondered where Frank thought the time was going.

It was just then that *she* walked by.

Paul did not think, he merely reacted. Reacted to the short black skirt, the long dark legs, the white gypsy blouse, the obvious push-up bra, the long shining black hair, the pride which showed in the way she carried her head. That beautifully shaped head! Paul reacted as she checked in at the bar by frantically signaling a nearby waiter. Don Frank came in and sat down just as the waiter came to the table. And Paul balked. "Bring a beer for my friend here," he said.

Frank looked surprised and then grinned. "You gonna buy me a beer? Man!"

"I'll be right back," said Paul, and he got up and went quickly up to the bar.

She was arranging something in her purse. There was a look of pure concentration on her face. The music started, very loud as usual. It made Paul tense. He tried to relax. He tapped her lightly on the shoulder. She looked at him, tilting her head back as she did so. Then she gave him that smile. The teeth were very white in the black-light glow of the bar.

"Hello," said Paul. He couldn't hear himself.

She turned towards him slightly, moving closer. Paul felt his arm sliding between her breasts. They felt soft and firm. She leaned her head up close to his mouth, the delicate ear that seemed so suddenly offered almost shocking him. The music was very loud.

"What is your name?" said Paul. His mouth was dry.

She spoke in a way that was somehow slow, almost haltingly, and at the same time confident. Directly into his ear along with her warm soft breath came the words, "My name is Rosie. I am new here. I saw you today. I remember. I do not have a, what you call it, a badge. Not yet."

"No number yet," said Paul, back into her ear.

"No, tonight is my first night here."

"Jesus Christ," said Paul.

"What?"

"I said will you sit with me?"

"Where do you sit?"

Paul pointed to his table. Frank grinned and waved back across the dance floor.

"Your friend?"

"Yeah."

"Okay," she said nodding. "I be there soon." She turned and walked back towards the head, still looking down in her purse.

"Who's the chick?" asked Frank.

"I saw her first!"

"Okay, okay. Is she new here?"

"Yeah." Paul lit a cigarette. He felt anything but calm.

"She's tough."

Paul smiled and nodded. He drank his beer deeply and took a drag on his smoke. He didn't look at his friend.

"Tall," said Frank.

"Yeah."

Frank shook his head, grinning. He said something Paul couldn't hear.

"Well, how'd it go with Linda?"

Frank gave Paul his satisfied look and told him that he'd be staying in town tonight.

"Don't be late to work," Paul told him.

CHAPTER 12

At 0600, just as it was really starting to get light outside, whoever had the Desk Watch would open the door that led from the office into the bunk room and lounge and turn on the lights. Then he would close the door and go back to the desk, sit down and speaking into the yellow intercom mike he would say, "Reveille, reveille. Everybody up to begin morning clean-up." Or he might say, "Rise and shine. Time to clean and shine." Whoever it was would always say something like that, making up his own words, and he would say them a little too loudly, because he'd been up himself since a quarter to four, sitting alone at the desk.

Now it was 0600, early in the morning, and the lights were on and Paul lay under the sheet in his bottom rack not yet ready to move. It was Monday morning and at oh seven-thirty his section would get off and have twenty-four hours before they came back to work. It was the Monday morning after the Friday night with Rosie, and now Paul was thinking about her. He had thought about her the whole weekend at work and he was glad he was getting off now.

He sat up in his rack and reached down and began to put on his shoes. He did not have to put on his socks or pants because he had slept in them as he always did when he was at work in case there was an emergency. When he was done putting on his shoes he stood up and put on his blue dungaree shirt and blue ball cap and then he lit his first cigarette of the day. He felt tired and knew he would until he had gotten off duty and eaten a good breakfast and taken a shower and had his first drink out in town. This was as it always was and it was fine with him, but today he also felt excited.

Frank looked like he was still sleeping and Paul went over to him and shook him by the shoulder until his eyes were open. Don Frank groaned at him and Paul went out into the barn. The drivers were already moving the trucks out of the barn and Paul got a push broom from the rack and began to sweep the floor.

There were twenty-two men in the Starboard Section of the crash crew that Paul belonged to, and now in the morning all except the section leader and the drivers began the chore of cleaning up. Sweep, swab and buff the floors of the bunk room, the little galley, the lounge, and hallway. The barn floor did not have to be buffed, only swept and swabbed, like the head. Everybody did their part of it and by seven-fifteen it was usually done. The Port Section would begin showing up around seven, dragging in in little groups after their weekend in town, to relieve the Starboard Section.

At 0730 everybody would line up in the now clean barn and listen to the Chief read the Plan Of The Day. Paul liked to hear the day plan but usually he had to read it for himself since the Chief always mumbled his words. It was always hard to keep from laughing when the Chief talked, but at morning quarters everybody was always too tired to laugh.

Then after Morning Quarters the little blue "nickel-snatcher" pulled up to take everybody up the hill to the barracks and the chow hall. It was a long slow ride up the hill, stopping here and there along the way to pick up others who were getting off work too. But by the time you finally got up the hill you were ready for a good hot breakfast and were beginning to finally come awake.

Paul ate with Don Frank and he had his usual three fried eggs and fried potatoes and two glasses of apple juice and two glasses of milk. He never drank coffee anymore, since San Miguel beer gave him enough trouble. He felt good after breakfast and even better after his *shit and shower.* He put on fresh civvie clothes, his old faded Levi's and a faded green tee-shirt with a pocket and his old dirty white sneakers and he was ready for town. He had two packs of Winston's that were as yet unopened and fifty-three pesos and it was nine-thirty in the morning and he was ready for whatever he would find out in town. He just wanted to hear her voice again.

The barracks were divided up into cubicles, which were made by squaring off sections of about four bunk-racks each with the tall lockers, and homemade plywood boxes that held stereo equipment and sea-bags filled with unused Navy Blues uniforms and stacks of saved up letters from home.

Don Frank was in his cube and he had his box open and was just putting on a tape in his cassette player. He had his earphones on and was still in his underwear after taking his shower and he hadn't even shaved yet.

Paul said, "I'm going into town."

Frank looked up at him and grinned. "Going to go see that chick, huh?"

"Rosie. Yeah, we made a date."

"Have fun. Never thought I'd see the day though."

84

"Don't make jokes. When are you going out?"

"Probably not until around four. Linda's still pissed off at me."

"Well, I'll be in the Sherry after five."

"Have fun," said Don Frank.

Paul arrived at Kong's at a quarter to ten and sat down at a table that he could see the door from. He wanted to be able to see her come in.

The waitress came and he ordered a Cuba Libre, which is a rum and coke with bitters or lime in it. It is a good drink to have in the tropics and after the first sip when it came Paul felt much better. It was cold and he savored each mouthful by holding it in his mouth before he swallowed it.

I hope she comes, he thought. Rosie. That she hasn't forgotten about me. I think she'll probably be late, but I just hope she comes. Man, I hope she comes. To have a woman like that here! Hell, anywhere! Even back in the States.

He was thinking of her and picturing her in his mind. Man, he thought, I hope she comes. If nothing else that's any good ever happens to me here, just let her happen. The way she looks, he thought. Her eyes, he thought. And the way her mouth looks from the side. The shape of her lips. If nothing else, I hope that she comes. Only that she comes. No, not that only. Because if she does show up, I'll want her. Damn, I want her now. I'd better control that kind of thing, he told himself. To go to bed with her today, in the afternoon, that would be something. Her fingers were so long and brown and the nails so long and white and sharp. So dark, her hands. I'd better stop thinking of it, he thought. Yes, I'd better.

He drank some more of his drink and looked at the clock on the wall behind him. It was half past ten now, and he lit another cigarette.

She came in finally through the glass door while he was lighting it and he saw her through the smoke, which burned his eyes and made him squint. She was wearing a short light brown skirt and a white blouse that had a ruffled collar with no sleeves and her hair was tied back in a long ponytail, like a schoolgirl. She had on large round blue sunglasses and long stockings almost up to her knees that made her legs look much lighter than they were. She saw him from where she was standing by the door and smiled. Her teeth were very clean looking and white.

She came over and sat down without saying anything. She took one of his Winston's from his pack on the table and he held the lighter for her. He felt very proud of her sitting with him.

"I did not think you would be here," she said.

"I didn't know if you would come," said Paul, and she looked away for a moment.

Then she looked back at him and said, "I was thinking I would come and nobody would be here in Kong's that I know."

"Well, I'm very glad you came," said Paul.

"You look very nice."

"I should have worn something better."

"No, you look very nice. Nice and clean. It is better for the woman to dress up, but for the man to look casual." She squeezed his knee under the table.

"What will we do?" she asked him.

"Whatever you want to do."

"Oh, I do not know."

"Are you hungry?"

"No," she said.

"You can have anything you want to eat."

"Thank you, but I am not hungry. Maybe later."

"Okay. Well, we could go to a movie," he told her.

"What is there to see?"

"I don't know."

"What is the movie on base?" she asked him.

"That's a good idea," he said. I'll take you on base. It's really a good movie. *Bullitt*. With Steve McQueen. Wait'll you see this one part of it. Best car chase ever."

"But I forgot," she said. "We can't go on base until four o'clock. They won't let you take me on base until four o'clock."

"Oh. Are you sure? I thought it was one o'clock."

"On weekends it is one o'clock."

"How do you know?"

"Because Saturday my friend went on base with a customer, and I asked her. I was thinking of this date with you."

"Oh," he said.

"Anyway," she said, "four o'clock is too late. I have to go to work at six."

"Oh," he said.

"Let's find a movie here in town."

"Okay."

"Just leave the money on the table for your drink," she told him and stood up.

"I paid for it already," he told her, and she smiled down at him.

They walked down the street in the hot sun towards the bridge and the gate. It was a very bright day and Paul put on his sunglasses. They made her look very dark. He loved the way she smelled. Especially her hair.

They walked not too slowly and she had her arm through his. She stopped and he stood looking at her. There were three movie theaters in that one small section, two across the street from them and one where they stood. She was looking across the street.

"Let's go there," she said, pointing.

The theater was right next to the money exchange and Paul knew about it without looking. "It's one of those *kung-fu* movies," he said to her.

"Good," she said, smiling brightly.

She led him across the street to the ticket window. There were stairs leading up to the ticket window and Paul went up these alone and asked for two tickets. When he turned around she was walking away.

"Wait! Where are you going?" he called.

She turned around and said, "Wait." He watched her go up the street through the crowd from the top of the stairs.

She was gone for about five minutes and Paul was nervous the whole time. But when she came back she had two bags of cheese flavored corn chips for them to eat during the movie.

"You didn't have to do that," he told her.

"Come on," she said, and they went up the stairs into the theater. She stopped at the candy counter and bought two cokes for them.

"Let me pay for them," said Paul.

"No," she told him, and gave the girl the money.

They were upstairs in the balcony part of the theater and it was very dark and hard to see after being outside. Paul put his sunglasses back in his shirt pocket, but Rosie just shoved hers up on her head. One of the movies was already playing and a young man with a flashlight seated them near the center aisle. On the screen there was a large blond girl that was naked from the waist up. She was pacing about in a cheap looking room, like she was agitated.

"She has big *susu*'s, eh?" said Rosie, nudging him with her elbow and laughing.

Paul thought the cheese things were very good. After a while Rosie put her hand on his thigh and slowly raked it with her long nails. She leaned her head on his right shoulder and he could feel her chewing the cheesy chips. Her hair smelled wonderful.

After the movies were over they went back outside into the sunlight and Rosie stopped by the curb. "What we do now?" she asked.

"I don't know," said Paul.

"It's still early."

"Yeah."

They stood there and a taxi pulled up, the driver thinking they were waiting for one. Rosie shook her head at him.

"Why don't we go to your house," said Paul.

"What! To my house?"

"Sure. You have a house, don't you?"

"I only have a room. It is very small."

"So?" said Paul, shocked at his daring.

She shrugged. "Okay, we go there. But I don't know why you want to."

"I only want to see how you live. I don't want any, you know...," said Paul.

They got into the taxi and Rosie said to the driver, "*Babuyan.*"

The driver did a U-turn and drove them out Magsaysay until it ended and then he went right on Rizal. Paul was wondering how far it would be to her house. They came to the traffic circle where the Victory Liner station was and turned left. It was the road that went out past Subic City and White Rock and on to San Miguel and the Lingayen Gulf. Paul knew this road from the time he and Frank had gone to San Miguel for the surf. But only a couple of blocks after they turned there was a bridge and the driver turned right on the first street after the bridge. Paul thought that some of the houses along this road looked pretty fancy, at least for houses in the Philippines. The road and the houses were along the slope of a green hill that ran by the river. Paul could see the river down below on his right.

They did not go far along this road before Rosie told the driver to stop. She let Paul pay the driver his Pesos.

It was a big house but Rosie had only one room in it. There was an older woman sitting outside on the covered porch, but she said nothing and hardly looked up from her knitting as they walked past. There was a padlock on the door in the hall. Rosie unlocked it and pushed the door open, then she kicked off her shoes and went in. There was a yellow bead curtain covering the doorway. Paul took off his sneakers before he went in. It was a square room with one single bed against the wall by the window, and another single bed placed in the corner next to it, making an L shape. Opposite from the beds there was a sort of open closet room and many clothes hung there. Next to the beds was a little table with a small mirror on it and next to that there were two wooden chairs and another little table between them. The floor was bare.

Rosie was leaning over slightly and looking at herself in the mirror. She had removed her large blue glasses and they sat now on the little table in front of her. Paul went over and sat in one of the chairs behind her.

Rosie looked at him in the mirror and said, "Would you like a beer?"

"Sure."

She went to the door and leaned her head out in the hall through the yellow beads and called out something in *Tagalog*. A boy came running and she said something to him and he left.

Rosie turned and began to unbutton her blouse. "Don't watch me," she said to Paul with a stern expression on her face.

On the little table in front of him there was a *Tagalog* Magazine. Paul picked it up and looked through it until he came to a section where the Filipino movie stars were, and he looked at these. Rosie was taking off her outer clothes over by the closet, her back to him. Paul looked at her now and then, secretly.

She took off everything except her white bra and her pink panties. She caught him looking once and said again, "Don't watch me." She didn't look at him when she said it but he could see a frown on her face.

Paul said, "I'm sorry. But you can't blame me."

"Oh?"

She put on a blue and white striped blouse that was very long. It buttoned down the front and she buttoned all but the top two buttons. Paul could see beads of sweat in the hollow of her smooth brown throat.

Rosie moved the chair that was next to his over in front of the little table and sat down. She was facing him now. She took a white handkerchief from her purse and wiped her throat and forehead with it.

"It's so damn hot," she said.

"I know," said Paul.

He watched her while she lifted her heavy hair and wiped the back of her neck.

The boy came with four cold bottles of beer and Rosie opened two of them. She put them on the table and got an ashtray from a shelf by the beds. She sat back down and got a deck of cards out of her purse and handed them to Paul. The cards were very old and were soft with age.

"What do you want to play?" asked Paul.

"Rummy."

Paul shuffled the cards as best he could and watched her drink hungrily from her beer. Her head was back as she drank and he watched her jaws and her throat working. Her eyes were open and looking towards the ceiling as she drank.

"I didn't know you liked beer," Paul said.

"All Filipinos like beer," she said. "But it makes me too fat."

"I don't think you're fat."

"You see my stomach? That is why I told you not to watch me."

"Maybe," said Paul. "But the rest of you. Fabulous!"

Rosie shrugged and looked at her cards.

"Why did you come here from Manila?" Paul asked.

"No more money there," said Rosie.

"There's lots of money here."

"Yes. That's why my sister brought me here."

"Your sister?"

"My sister lives here too."

"I didn't know you had a sister."

"Yes. Her name is Margaret."

"Does she look like you?"

"We are just the same. But her hair is short. She works in the Sherry Club too."

"I haven't seen her," said Paul.

Rosie made her haughty expression. "I would not let her come near you," she said. Then she laughed and smiled. "Because I know you are a *butterfly*."

"I'm not," said Paul.

"You have a girl in the states? Maybe a wife?" She was smiling at him.

"No. Maybe a girlfriend, but no wife."

"I never go to bed with a married man, anyway."

"Never?"

"No, never. Nor my sister. It is one of our rules."

"Oh," said Paul.

"We have many rules."

"I'll bet you do."

"I never give blowjob in my life," said Rosie, with her haughty expression again.

"I wish you wouldn't talk like that," Paul told her.

"Why? Is it wrong? I am what I am."

"I know," said Paul.

"Anyway, if you don't like it..." She let her voice drop off.

"Don't worry about what I like," said Paul. "So why did you and your sister come here?"

"Because there is no more money in Manila. You see, my sister and I, we are from close by to Manila. Our mother lives there with our little brother. Margaret and I worked in the Whiskey A Go-Go for a long time. Then they closed the R and R center and there is no more money."

"I didn't know there was an R and R center there," said Paul.

"For Marines and soldiers from Vietnam. But because of Expo 70 in Japan they close it down."

"Oh."

"So, Margaret come here to look this town over. She heard there was much money here. I never heard of this place before she told me. But we don't like it here. We want to go back to Manila someday."

"There's a lot of money here."

"Not so much. Not like Manila before they close the R and R center."

"Well, money's not everything," said Paul.

Rosie shrugged. "Money is not too important to me."

"I'll bet," said Paul, making it a joke.

"Well, I am expensive. You want to know how much I can charge someone?" She looked at him with an odd expression he hadn't seen before. "Maybe a thousand Pesos, altogether. Maybe more."

"That's a lot. I couldn't pay it."

"No?" Rosie laughed a little and gave him her expression. "Then you wouldn't get it."

"I thought you said money wasn't important to you."

"A woman like me, she must think of her pride."

"You have a lot of pride."

"One time in Manila, a Marine came to the club and pointed to me. The manager told him how much, and the Marine said it was okay. There in Manila it is different. You pay for one whole week with the girl in advance. It cost much money. Eight hundred dollars altogether. The club gets half of this. Anyway, the Marine said okay. So, I go with him. The R and R center has a room for him in the Manila Hilton. Very fancy place. It is late, so this Marine and I, we go to the room. His name was Larry. From Texas, I think. Anyway, I ask him, why we don't go barhopping. He say he is tired. So we go to the room. Then he say to me, why don't you take off your clothes. I tell him to turn off the light, but he say no, he likes it better with the light on. He takes off his clothes and sits on the bed. He says, come here Rosie. So, I walk over in front of him. What do you want, I ask him. He is ugly with no clothes. He say, you know what I want. I want you to do something for me. I know what he wants, but I say, what do you want? So he tells me, come on Rosie, put your mouth here. I say, never. Never! Never will I do that. Not to any man. So he gets mad. Come on, he says. What do you think you are? I tell him I will do anything but that, if he turns off the lights. Now he say, you are a bitch. A whore. I slap him, very hard, and he gets up and hits me. With his fist! Three times, he hits me. So I run away, I leave, I go home. Next day, the manager comes to see me. He is very mad, but when he sees my face he gets very sorry and angry too. He is Chinese, anyway. But he says I cannot work in his club anymore, because the Marine reported me to the R and R center. I get very mad now. I go to the officer there, and I ask him, where is this man who reports me for stealing his money. Here is his damn money. The officer had this Larry called in, and right in front of him I tell the officer what happened. The officer is looking at my face. So then they give me the money back."

"What did they do to the guy?" asked Paul.

"They sent him back to Vietnam. I think they busted him too."

"Well, he deserved whatever they did to him. That must have been something, though, in front of that officer."

"I had to stay out of work for a month, because of my face," said Rosie.

They sat and played cards in the heat and Paul thought about the life this girl was living. This woman, he thought.

Margaret came home that afternoon just as Rosie was starting to put on her make-up to go to work. She did not look *just like* Rosie, not from the neck up anyway, but Paul did not point that out. He felt that maybe he was being tested somehow, tested by Rosie and her sister, and he was taking things easy.

Margaret had short curly cropped hair, and a rounder face than Rosie. Her cheekbones were fairly high, and even though her skin was lighter than her sisters, she looked more *Negroid* to Paul than anything else he could think of. She was very pretty and friendly and had a quicker sense of humor than her sister. Paul liked her right away.

She sat and talked to him while Rosie carefully applied her layers in front of the mirror, ignoring them. Or seemingly ignoring us, thought Paul. I'll bet she's listening to every word.

Margaret was telling him about her boyfriend, who only two weeks before had gone back to the States.

"He was married, you know," said Margaret.

"I didn't guess," said Paul, echoing her humorous tone.

"Yes, he had a wife in Texas. He loved her very much, I think."

"That's good."

"Sometimes I was jealous of her," said Margaret.

"Was he nice?"

"He was very nice. Nicer than you, maybe. Rosie will tell me how nice you are, but I think maybe he was nicer than you. Not enough time to tell about you, yet."

"I'm very nice," said Paul.

"No joke. He was very good to me, and to my sister. Every time he come to see us, he bring present. And every payday he give me ten dollars."

"What kind of presents did he give you?"

"Oh, you know. Like eye make-up from the base, or shampoo sometimes. He was very nice."

"Ten dollars every payday, huh?"

"Sometimes fifteen. To help pay the rent."

"I thought you guys just came to Olongapo," said Paul.

"This was in Manila," said Margaret. "He was from Sangley."

"Oh."

"And you know, we hate this town already. Very bad here. The people are not nice. Not even to us. The way we speak, you know, they can tell we are from Manila."

"Rosie was telling me," said Paul. He looked at her. She glanced away from the mirror long enough to grin at him, then looked back at her image again. Paul thought she looked terrible already, with all that junk on her face. The make-up was for the clubs, he knew.

"This is a very bad town," Margaret was saying. "Even for us. You know how this town is. You know the way the taxi drivers try to ask for more money? Well, this does not happen in Manila."

"I've never been in Manila," said Paul.

"Sometime maybe Rosie and I will take you."

"Hah!" said Rosie, grinning. "Maybe if he is nice enough to me." She laughed.

"She is only joking with you," said Margaret. "She is like that, always thinking she is funny. But you are nice. I can tell." She said something to Rosie in *Tagalog*.

"Hah!" said Rosie. She laughed, looking at Paul. "You know what she said? She said, 'You better be nice to this man. He is very good looking.' So I say now, what do I care if he is good looking? Maybe he better be good in bed, too." She laughed again at this.

"See what I mean?" said Margaret. "Always thinking she is funny."

Paul smiled.

"Anyway," said Margaret after a while, "I am very sad now that my boyfriend is gone. Not about the money, but because he was so nice. He was married, you know, so I never could sleep with him. It is one of our rules, to never go with a married man. But he was very understanding about that. Every payday he gave me ten dollars, to help with the rent. Just because he liked me and Rosie."

"What would happen if you had a customer at the house when he came?" asked Paul.

"We never bring customers to the house. Another rule. Did you know that since we have been here, you are the first man to come to this house?"

"No," said Paul.

"Yes. And you want to know another of our rules?"

"Sure," said Paul.

"Okay. If one man, one boyfriend of mine, does something to hurt me, then later Rosie will take care of him. We do not tell *customers* we are sisters, you know. Then, same thing if someone hurts Rosie. I get him." She opened her purse and took out a curved folding knife and opened it. ""You know what this kind of knife is called?" she asked him.

"It's a Butterfly knife," said Paul.

"That's right. So, you better not be Butterfly to my sister." She laughed.

"I don't know if she even wants me yet," said Paul. He grinned and looked at Rosie. She gave him her snobbish look, then grinned when she looked back into the mirror.

"You are the first to know we are sisters," said Margaret. "The other night Rosie ask me if it is okay to tell you. To bring you to the house. I say, 'Rosie, it is up to you, because if you want to make him your boyfriend, then he should know.'"

"Hah!" said Rosie. She muttered something in *Tagalog*.

"Then you better not listen," Margaret said to her. "She thinks I tell you too much," she said to Paul.

"I don't think so," said Paul, grinning. He felt better than he had ever felt in his life, even if there was nervousness in his stomach.

"You should not tell anyone we are sisters," said Margaret.

"I promise not to tell a soul."

"Good," said Margaret.

Later Paul stood outside the house in the street and waited until an empty taxi came by. It was about five-thirty and it was starting to get dark. When a taxi came, he called, and Rosie came out of the house all dressed for work. She looked truly beautiful in the blue twilight. Paul was glad he'd asked her to have dinner first.

In the taxi she sat close to him, and he put his arm up on the seat behind her head, letting his hand rest on her shoulder.

After a while she said, "Don't listen too much to Margaret. Her boyfriend was a second-class Petty Officer. I know you do not make so much money as him. But if every night you come in the taxi and pick me up for work?"

Paul explained that he could not do this every night, because of the way his working days were arranged.

"I know this. But if you want to do it when you are in town."

"I will," said Paul.

"It will be very nice of you," said Rosie. "And if you could bring a pack of Salem's when you come."

Paul nodded. Then he said, "What are you telling me, Rosie?"

She looked at him with her dark eyes, smiling.

Paul pulled her closer to him. He wanted to kiss her, but he didn't just then.

Rosie said, "And in the club, when you come, I will sit with you. You only have to buy me one drink, and I will sit all night with you. The manager is very mean about the drinks. But I will not drink the one drink, I will just let it sit. He has many girls to watch, and he will be fooled."

"That's very smart," said Paul.

Rosie looked away. Then she squeezed his hand.

After dinner at Kong's they went into the Sherry Club. Rosie went to the bar to check in. She'd told Paul that she would join him later, but that they must not walk in together, so Paul waited a little time outside, before he went in.

Frank was inside, sitting at the usual table near the wall by the stage. Paul sat down and ordered a beer.

"Well, how'd it go?" asked Frank, grinning.

"What do you mean, how'd it go? It went fine."

"I saw her come in. How was she?"

"What do you mean, how was she? She's fine."

"I mean in bed."

"We didn't go to bed," said Paul, having decided not to lie.

"You didn't go to bed?"

"No. No, not yet. I'm going to wait for her to decide when."

"You mean you're going to wait until she asks for it?"

"You could put it that way."

"Don't hold your breath. She's a working girl."

"One of these times she will decide," Paul told him.

"I wouldn't hold my breath," said Don Frank.

"Here she comes." Goddamn, he thought. Just look at her.

She was coming past the bar and into the soft yellow light of the empty dance floor. She was wearing a short black dress and black shoes and her hair was hanging long, back from her shoulders. She walked with grace, steadily, with her head up and tilted back just a little. She looked very proud of herself, and as she walked towards Paul she smiled at him, and she looked very happy.

She pulled the chair around close to him and sat down, crossing her legs, and putting her hand on his arm. She leaned over and whispered in his ear that Margaret liked his friend. "She told me the other night," she said.

Paul had gotten chills from her breath in his ear, and now he grinned because of them. But then he said, whispering back in her ear, "He sort of has a girlfriend already. But they've been fighting lately, so I don't know. I'm sure he'd like Margaret, though."

Rosie told him that from now on to wait until she came, before he ordered a beer. The manager would like that better, she told him, and. besides, she got a commission.

Paul told her to go get a drink for herself and another beer for him. She smiled and got up and went to the bar for the drinks. It came to nearly ten Pesos. Frank looked surprised that Paul would buy a drink for any girl.

"Only for this one," Paul told him, while she was gone. "Besides, I only have to buy her one drink."

The music started after a while, and they danced. Frank wanted to dance with her too, and Paul let him. It didn't bother him.

Rosie hardly touched her drink all that night, drinking out of his beer instead, every now and then. She seemed to get drunk after a while. Not really drunk, but playful. She began after a while to slide her long painted white nails up and down the inside of his thigh. Teasing him, he decided. But it was playful teasing, and he didn't really mind it.

Don Frank left after a couple of hours to go patch things with Linda across the street. He told Paul he would be back later. Paul didn't mind him going at all. It gave him a chance to move to a back table with Rosie, and to kiss her long and deeply, as he had been wanting to do ever since he had seen her the very first time.

He went back on base that night very happy.

CHAPTER 13

They passed the months together that way. On his days off, Paul would go every evening before six in a cab to her house and pick her up and take her to work. She would go inside first, so that the manager would not see them coming in together, and then Paul would go in and sit at his usual table and wait for her to come to him. She would always come, bringing him a beer, and unless she had a customer she would sit the whole night with him. When she did have a Fleetie customer, she could not spend the whole time with Paul, but she would come every half hour or so and say a few words and smile and sometimes make him dance with her. And when she had such a customer Paul did not mind. Not too much, anyway. She had to work. Make money. He understood that. It was just like Frank and Linda, wasn't it? So, when she had a Fleetie customer she would sit with him, and dance with him, and smile the same way she did when she was with Paul.

And Paul would sit and involve himself in the music and try not to pay any attention to the ache in his gut. The worst times were the times that she left with a customer, went outbar-hopping for a few hours with him. They were the worst times because Paul would have to look at the empty face of the sailor when they came back. The empty face that seemed to mean only one thing. And the bored look, the tired look, on Rosie's face. Usually when she left Paul got up and went over to the New Life Club. Usually he could smoke some weed over there, and Don Frank would be there also, since Linda would likely be with a customer too.

Tonight though, there were no ships in. No fleetie's with thirty days at sea worth of combat pay to blow. No real business for the hostess girls. If their slack periods lasted more than three or four days the town itself would start to starve. But Paul liked these quiet times best of all. He could have Rosie to himself, and not have to share her with some sailor. Usually Margaret would sit with them at the table and they would talk until closing time, talking of many things, little things and big things. And when Frank wasn't with Linda, he'd be sitting with them too, talking.

But tonight, Don Frank wasn't there. And Margaret had not come to work. Paul sat alone at his table in the front by the band and waited for Rosie to come out of the dressing room in the back of the club. It was early, only a little after seven, and the guys in the band were still setting up their equipment. Even Eto looked bored tonight. The club was nearly empty, except for the half a dozen or so girls that had shown up for work. Paul somehow felt nervous waiting. There were only two other Americans in the club, and they sat alone in the back by the wall, drinking.

If I dance with her tonight, Paul thought, those two dudes will have nothing better to do than watch. They won't be able to *not* watch from where they're sitting. If only I wasn't such a spaz dancing. I wonder why Rosie even dances with me? Well, she does. That's enough, isn't it? Sure it is. I guess I dance okay when I don't try too hard. Anyway, it doesn't matter.

I wish she'd come out of there. Those dudes will blow their minds when they see what a beauty I've got sitting with me. Sure they will.

When Rosie came out of the dressing room in the back Paul saw that she wore the short black skirt and the same white low-cut gypsy blouse that she'd worn months ago, the first night they'd met. She came across the dance floor and her dark brown skin looked even darker under the soft yellow light.

She had not been in a very good mood when Paul had picked her up for work that evening, but now she was smiling brightly and she seemed to move almost playfully. She arched her head back and looked down at Paul, standing at his side but just a little behind him, so that he had to turn his head around to see her properly. He smiled up at her.

"Well," she said, "are you going to buy something to drink? Or are you broke again tonight?" She smiled coyly, teasing.

"Come off it," said Paul grinning. "I told you in the cab I had some coin tonight. If you think I should buy you a drink, then I will. I don't mind. I'll have a beer."

Rosie held out her hand.

Paul pulled, out his wallet. "Well?" he said. He did not like her holding out her hand like that in front of the two guys in the back. He could imagine them snickering.

Rosie said, "You know the manager makes me ask for a drink. If you don't want to buy me one, then I can sit alone. I don't care."

Paul handed her a twenty Peso bill. He felt angry. They'd been through this so many times before. He wanted to say, Rosie, you know I don't mind the money, but don't make such a spectacle out of asking for it. But he didn't say it, not this time. Instead he smiled coolly. Rosie smiled back, softly he thought, and then she walked towards the bar.

The music started. Hard rock. Paul relaxed in the sound. It was very loud. Nobody would be able to hear what he was thinking.

Rosie came back and sat down with her drink and Paul drank deep and long from his beer. His mouth had been so dry. When he put the beer down on the table Rosie picked it up and took a long drag on it herself. Then she smiled at him and laughed. She laughed for what seemed quite a while, making him curious. Paul lit a cigarette for her and one for himself. They sat listening to the music.

After a while Don Frank came in, bringing Linda with him. It was the first time Paul had seen them together in the Sherry Club. But the two girls had met before, one afternoon in Ding's, and now they began to chatter in Tagalog. Eto up on the stage was putting a new string on his guitar. Frank went up and asked him to play some blues. Paul could see Eto grinning and nodding his head. It must be good to know you have an audience that cares, he thought.

Don Frank asked Rosie to get a couple of beers for him and Linda, and Rosie hurried up to the bar.

Frank said, "She seems in a good mood tonight."

Paul nodded, grinning. He felt silly doing it.

Linda smiled. "She said she is happy tonight, because her boyfriend is very good to her."

Paul felt himself blush.

"Oh!" said Don Frank. He laughed and nudged Paul on the shoulder.

"Yeah. Shit," said Paul, but he was still smiling broadly.

Rosie came back with the beers and Frank gave her five Pesos. She walked back to the bar and got her plastic coin voucher. When she came back she sat down and put her arm around Paul's neck and squeezed very hard and kissed him near his ear. Paul felt himself blushing deeply.

Then the music started and Don Frank and Linda got up to dance. Frank motioned for Paul and Rosie to join them. Rosie pulled on Paul's arm and they got up and went out on the floor. It was a long slow blues dance, featuring the electric guitar, and Paul tried to let himself flow with it, holding Rosie in his arms. The two dudes in the back, Paul noticed, now had two girls with them. They weren't paying any attention to him, not now. He relaxed more.

Rosie moved warmly against him, her long legs pressing against one of his thighs whenever they turned a certain way. Her eyes were closed, and he could feel her warm breath on his neck, and her soft black hair was clinging against his face.

When the song was over they sat back down and now Rosie sat closer to him, her hand on his thigh.

Don Frank said, "What are you guys doing tomorrow?"

"Why?" asked Rosie.

"We are going to White Rock," said Linda.

"Yeah," said Don Frank. "You guys ought to go with us."

Paul felt Rosie squeeze his hand. He looked at her. "How would you like that?" he asked.

"Okay," she said smiling. "If you have enough money."

Frank laughed.

"What time?" asked Paul.

"I guess about nine or ten," said Frank. "We'll take a Jeepney up there."

Rosie said, "Pick us up at the house. You know where the house is?"

"Yeah, okay," said Don Frank.

Paul looked at Rosie and felt himself starting to smile. She looked back at him with an expression that said, *don't act like a kid about it.*

"How do you know where her house is?" said Linda, playfully.

"Uh oh," said Frank. He grinned at Paul.

"I took him with me out there a couple of times," said Paul.

"Anyway, pick us up at my house," Rosie said.

"Okay," said Don Frank. "That's a deal then."

"Man," said Paul, under his breath, and he felt Rosie hit him in the leg. But when he looked at her she was smiling.

That night was the first time. The first time Paul went home with Rosie after the club closed. Margaret gave up her bed and went out to sleep on the floor in the hall. It was the first time she'd ever had to do that, but she didn't seem to mind. Rosie said it was the first time any man had ever spent the night at her house. She made him take a shower first, and he washed his mouth of the beer taste with the water. When he was done he waited naked and alone in the bed, under the single light blanket, while Rosie had her shower. He waited and his mind raced incomprehensibly. His one thought that he couldn't escape was the fact that he'd had an erection since they'd gotten in the cab to come home, and he'd had quite a time hiding this fact from her.

Now he waited and felt himself shaking. He didn't want to fail. All of his experience with women seemed useless to him now. It had to be good, meaning that it had to be good for her, that was all that mattered. He was shaking.

But then she came out and closed the door, and took off the towel, and was naked in the light from the window, and he stopped shaking. Then she was in the bed, and the blanket was gone, and her hair was hanging down on his face, and he could think no more.

CHAPTER 14

They were out on Hardstand Duty. The runway was about twenty yards ahead of them. Just then at the far end of the runway, which was the usual approach end of two five, an F-4 Phantom was lining up for take-off. Paul, sitting up on the back of the yellow Oshkosh crash truck, watched through his binoculars.

The two white helmeted men, the one in front the pilot and the one behind him the navigator, had closed their canopies. The light gray, almost white painted Navy jet came to a stop in the center of the runway and began to turn up its powerful twin jet engines. As Paul watched it began to roll slightly, the pilot having released his brakes. Then came the far-off boom of the after-burners igniting, and the Phantom began to really roll. It passed the Hardstand strip at well over two hundred and fifty knots, flames caused by the afterburners steadily shooting out, roaring so loudly that Paul and the others on the truck covered their ears. It was always a surprise how loud those aircraft were, thought Paul. No matter if you expected great loudness or not. It was always louder than you expected.

Paul looked at his watch. It was 0340. He looked back across the taxi-way behind him towards the Crash House barn. Yes, the chow truck was already here. In five minutes or so Cubi 4 would be out to relieve them from the Hardstand. Paul could hardly wait. He was hungry, and anyway he could look forward to not having to work anymore that afternoon. Unless they had a hot-drill tonight or an emergency or something. But that wasn't really the same as drudge work. They wouldn't have to wax any trucks or swab any floors or any of the other busy work that Smith was always thinking up for them during working hours. But mainly Paul was glad to be going in because it would give him a chance to talk to Don Frank. He hadn't had a chance to talk to Frank since they had started work that morning. Not really converse with him. To find out what Rosie had had to say last night.

Rosie. He tried thinking of her the same way he had thought of other girls that he had known and loved. Certain other girls he thought he had loved. But do I love Rosie? Really love her? He thought that he was a fool if he did. And. if he did, he thought that he would never tell her. Or anyone else. Like Don Frank, for instance. But Rosie was something. Really something. Everyone thought so. She and her sister had been in Olongapo City for nearly 10 months now, and there were many other station guys after her. He could not be out in town every day. Paul had even heard that some guy in the Port section of the crash crew was the one that was *really* her boyfriend. Paul wondered about that. What did that mean? And who could it be if it was true? There was really no way he could know, not for sure anyway, since nobody in the Port Section was *ever* in town at the same time the Starboard duty section was. Paul had been her so-called *station sailor boyfriend* for almost the whole time she'd been here. He had heard her telling people that herself. But now, with this latest fight they'd had, he did not know. Paul sighed and then lit a cigarette. If only she wasn't so damned, so damned...what was the word he wanted? *Proud.* That was the word she used.

Inside the truck the radio crackled. Then came a voice that Paul recognized as being that of Leonard, the fat driver of Cubi 4. "Cubi tower, this is Cubi 4, now on Hardstand." Paul turned around and watched the big yellow firetruck pulling up behind him. He heard the sound of the big diesel engine firing in the back of his own truck.

"Roger four," said the mildly laconic voice from the tower. "Cubi 6, you're cleared around the corner."

Cubi 6, the Oshkosh truck that Paul rode, headed out and turned left on the runway and then turned left at the midfield crossing again and returned to the Crash House barn.

Paul jumped off the back of the truck just before it came to a stop and went to the chow truck, a converted milk truck like van, and got his paper plate full of roast beef and mashed potatoes and green salad and two cartons of milk and went into the lounge and sat in a folding chair at the ping pong table to chow down.

When he was done eating he threw his plate and the empty cartons of milk in the trash can and went into the Head and relieved himself. He knew Don Frank had the desk-watch in the office, but he also knew that there were probably others in the office, and that Frank would call for him when they could talk freely. Paul went back through the lounge into the bunk-room and climbed up into his rack, after taking off his shirt and his shoes. Nobody said anything to him and the air-conditioning felt wonderful after the hot three hours out on the runway at Hardstand, and so he went to sleep.

Don Frank looked at the big electric clock on the wall above the window next to his desk. It was 1830. He picked up the yellow Crash House intercom mike, pushed down the black button and spoke into it, his voice low, his mouth very close to the mike. The words echoed back to him from the speaker in the lounge bunk-room next to the office. "Paul Sutton to the office."

Someone yelled from the lounge through the closed door that Paul was asleep.

"Wake his ass up," Frank yelled back.

A few minutes later Paul came through the door, shirtless and with his sunburned face wrinkled from sleep. "I figured you'd use that damn mike to wake me up," he said. "I knew you'd call me sooner or later." He sat down in the chair facing the desk.

"I had quite a talk with Rosie last night," said Frank, grinning.

Paul lit a cigarette and looked at his friend. He looked away and sighed. Then he said, "Did you call and order the baggies yet?"

"Yeah," said Frank. "I didn't forget to do it this time. Smith was already in here bugging me a while ago about it."

"Smith," said Paul.

"He's a sweat just like you," said Frank, grinning again.

"I'm not a sweat," said Paul. "I just worry about you."

Frank smiled. "I wonder what I would do without you to worry about me."

Paul looked out the window next to him into the darkness of the Philippine night. He could see the blue taxiway lights and the green and white beacon on the carrier pier going around and around. He could see the yellow marker lights of the Hardstand truck out by the runway. Cubi 4 was still on the job. He turned back to Frank. "Well, what did she say?"

"Maybe you'd better ask me what I said to her first," Don Frank told him, grinning secretively.

"Oh, I can guess what you told her," said Paul.

"I told her that you were 'on her side'."

"What? Okay, that's good. That's fine," said Paul.

"I told her that you weren't mad at her."

Paul nodded.

"I told her that the only problem with you was that you didn't *understand* her. That she had to make herself *clearer*. Make it easier for you to understand her."

"Yeah, okay. What did she say?" said Paul.

"She said that she missed you. She said that during this last week that you had been fighting that she hasn't been very happy."

Paul laughed. "Then why," he asked, "hasn't she talked to me?"

"She said that was because she was *too proud*. She says she is too proud, but there is nothing she can do about it."

They both laughed.

"Far out man. These girls here," said Paul, "are all way far-out. But she takes the cake. Rosie is the winner of the far-out badge."

Frank laughed and started to say something, but the radio interrupted him.

"Cubi tower, Cubi 4. Radio check." It was Fat Leonard again.

"Cubi 4, tower. Read you loud and clear. How me?"

"Loud and clear tower. Thank you."   Paul thought Leonard's voice had a little disappointment in it.

"The boys are getting restless out there," he told Frank.

Frank nodded., "There hasn't been any traffic, not a single aircraft taking off or landing in over an hour now. The tower should secure them."

"Those guys in the tower suck," said Paul. "I've sat out there for three hours before, and never seen traffic one, but the tower just forgets about us."

"Which reminds me," said Frank. "It's time for those guys to get relieved." He picked up the yellow intercom mike again and spoke into it, "Cubi 5 mount up, take up the strip. Cubi 5 mount up for Hardstand."

"Who's riding your truck while you're on watch?" asked Paul.

"Nobody.   We got an extra man, so we're not short.   That new guy, whatshisname."

"Oh yeah," said Paul.

Outside through the window they could see the crew of Cubi 5 walking past towards their truck. None of them looked happy. The driver, named Small, looked as though he had been asleep.

The radio crackled again. "Hardstand, tower. You're secured. Cleared around the corner." There was a pause, then. "Cubi one, Cubi tower."

Frank pushed down the button on the gray mike in front of him. "Cubi tower, this is Cubi one, go ahead."

"Uh, roger one. No further traffic expected for approximately 30 minutes to an hour. Expecting Charlie one forty-one from Clark. Inform Hardstand crew to be on two minutes notice."

"Roger tower," said Frank. He entered the fact that the Hardstand. had been secured in the logbook. Outside the window the crew of Cubi 5 walked past again, looking happier this time. Cubi 4 was making its way back towards the barn.

"Well," said Paul. "What else did she say?"

"Not much," said Frank. "But I talked to Margaret too."

"I've talked to her," said Paul. "She's no help."

Frank shrugged. "Let me have one of your Winston's," he said.

Paul gave him the cigarette and lit another one for himself. He was tired. Tired of the PI. Tired of the crash crew. But tomorrow he would go see Rosie. "What did Margaret say?" he asked Frank.

"She said that she thought Rosie was trying to change herself but doesn't know how. She said Rosie is very unsure of herself."

"One of these days," said Paul.

"What?" asked Frank.

Paul smiled. "Nothing," he said. "Nothing at all."

The door that led into the barn opened and Chief Morgan, the civil service fire captain came in. He was a very large, big boned man who was just starting to go to fat. He reminded Paul of Hoss Cartwright.

"Well," he said in his deep booming voice, "I see that the Hardstand is secured." He sat down heavily in one of the green plastic and gray metal chairs of the office.

"The tower says a C-141 is coming in pretty soon," said Frank. "Put us on two-minute notice.

Chief Morgan nodded. "Well, we might be busy tonight anyway."

Paul and Frank both groaned.

"We just had a hot-drill the other day Chief," said Paul.

"That was two weeks ago," said Chief Morgan, grinning.

"Ahhh..." said Paul.

The Chief laughed. "Got you worried huh? Nah, but we haven't had a grid-map drill for a long time. Well, we haven't needed one really. But now we got three or four new men, well..."

"In the morning," said Paul. "Have it in the morning. About oh-five-thirty. I won't mind getting up a half hour early for the benefit of the new men."

The Chief laughed.

"Yeah," said Don Frank. "Have it in the morning. Be a good guy Chief."

The Chief nodded and smiled. "Well, we'll see. But don't say nothing to anybody." He got up from the chair. "Well, guess I oughta call the wife."

The phone, the red phone that hung on the wall next to Frank, began its' loud incessant ring. It would ring steadily until answered. Both Paul and the Chief Morgan were out of the office, the door not yet closed behind then, by the time Frank picked up the receiver. Into his ear came the voice of someone in the tower.

"...all stations acknowledge when called. Cubi operations."

"Standing by," said the operations duty officer.

"Crash fire," said the tower.

"Standing by," said Frank.

Paul ran to the truck, opened the door to the cab and jumped in. He started the engines and turned on the radio, which was for the moment still silent. He began pulling on the pants of his fire-resistant silver suit. He almost had them on before the rest of the crew got out to the truck. The driver and the two rescue men. Then Paul realized with a great feeling of stupidity that he was riding Turret, that he had been for the last three duty days, and that he didn't need his pants. Just the jacket.

The rescue men jumped on the back of the truck. Paul could see Tony and Bill pulling on their suits through the back window. The driver of his truck, a tall thin fellow named Larry Walter, jumped in the truck behind the wheel, grinned up at Paul, and said, "Here we go." He flicked on the running lights and the red revolving beacon and drove out of the barn, flooring it.

Paul was knocked backwards, but he regained his balance, and as the truck headed for its position at three-quarter field, he stood up on the water pump cowling, pushed open the hatch, and took his position standing in the open hatchway behind the gray metal turret foam/water gun. He held on with one hand and with the other reached for the pin that held the turret gun from swinging freely by itself and pulled it out. He was ready. He heard the radio crackle and stuck his head down to hear over the roar of the wind.

"Cubi one, this is Cubi two," came the voice of Chief Morgan. "What's the nature of the emergency?"

"We have an inbound Charlie one forty-one with a stuck landing gear," said Frank in an awe-struck voice. "Also reports starboard engine failure. Both starboard engines."

The Chief in Cubi two, did not answer.

Having reached its position at three quarter field, Cubi 6 came to a stop, its engine running and its red-lights flashing. Down the field Paul could see three other red flashing lights in the darkness, at various positions along the runway.

Then over the radio came Chief Morgan's' voice once more.

"Cubi tower, this is Cubi two. What is the ETA on that bird?"

"Cubi two, Cubi tower. About five minutes." The voice in the tower sounded resigned.

"Can you get him to hold?"

"Pilot says he's got smoke in the cockpit, he's losing cabin pressure and he can't get a wheels down and locked indication. He's inbound from Da Nang, by the way."

"Why won't Clark take him?"

"Runways at Clark are closed by fog," the tower said.

"Jesus Christ," said Paul. "Walter, this is going to be a big one. There's never been a crash at Cubi like this one." Actually, there'd been none at all during his time here.

Larry Walter shook his head. "Better tell the guys in the back what's up so they won't fall off the truck when that thing creams in here. God."

Paul put his head back up through the hatch thinking that the vacation was over.

Over the radio came the words from somewhere, the voice unknown. "Shit, we're in for it now."

Neither Paul nor Larry Walter laughed. Paul did not think anybody anywhere could possibly think it was very funny.

Out in the distance towards the mouth of the bay, possibly just over Grande Island, they could see the lights of the approaching cargo plane. The wheel lights were showing and Paul felt a great amount of relief.

The tower said, "The pilot informs us he wishes to come straight in. We have informed him his wheel lights are showing in the two main mounts. However, no light showing in his nose gear. We have also informed him that the runway has not been foamed."

"Thank you tower," said the Chief in Cubi two.

Paul could see the red flashing light of the Chief's little red pickup sitting just in front of the Hardstand truck. This was going to be bad. He thought it would be much better if the plane had already crashed and they had had no warning. That way there would have be no time to sweat about it.

The big cargo transport plane seemed to come in slowly, it's two remaining engines making a great deal of noise as they strained to keep the great weight in the air. Paul sensed rather than heard the squeal of the main landing wheels as it touched gently down, her pilot in supreme control. The it came down the runway much faster than Paul liked. He could see the other crash trucks turn out onto the runway behind the giant aircraft to follow it, their lights flashing and sirens blaring. The aircraft was almost to three quarters field before the pilot, seen now as a dark shadow in the lit cockpit, allowed the nose of the plane to touch gently down.

Sparks flew everywhere. The loudest screeching noise that Paul had ever heard flew wildly in the warm night air. The plane shot past them, but Paul could see it was slowing radically now, the roar of reversing engines blended with the screeching of metal and the howling of the sirens of the other crash trucks. Paul had to grab wildly at the handle of the turret to keep from being thrown off his feet as Larry Walter sped the truck down on to the runway to follow the aircraft.

The plane spun sideways, the port wing tip nearly scraping the ground, and then it came to a sudden halt, the pilots immediately shutting the engines down. The crewmen were already piling out through the rear door, the big cargo door, which Paul thought the pilot must have opened, or ordered open, long before touchdown.

The plane did not explode or catch fire, much to everyone's satisfaction, but the Air Force crew still got out of the plane in a big hurry. Paul thought that he would have done the same.

It took them, along with the help of Runway Support, until sunrise to get the big plane cleared off the runway.

CHAPTER 15

I t was raining heavily when Paul arrived in the taxi at Rosie's house up on the hill on the other side of the river behind Olongapo. He paid the driver his Pesos and hurried under the protection of his small black Navy issue umbrella through the silver metal gate and into the shelter of the patio. It was a dark day, the sky hung heavy and black with low thick, wet clouds that moved quickly across the sky, never ending, never changing. The rain came heavily down, cool and persistent, through the warm humid air.

Paul could see the padlock on the door and he knew then that neither Rosie nor Margaret were home. And there was no childish scrawl of a note on the door, as there had been other times to leave a clue as to when or where they had gone. Paul stood in the outside doorway of the hallway. He did not know what to do. The Mama-San of the house sat in the old bamboo chair in the covered patio, smiling at him. Every time he had seen her, she had been smiling.

"The girls that live in that room," said Paul to her. "Rosie and Mar, do you know where they have gone? Have they gone to the market?"

The old lady was brown and wrinkled, her teeth brown and rotten looking. Her hair was straight and it was almost white and it was pulled back into a tight bun on the back of her head. She shook her head. "They did not come home last night. Mar told me that she and Rosie were going to Manila last night."

"To Manila?" said Paul.

"Yes. To see their mother they went to Manila," said the old lady, nodding and smiling.

Paul caught another taxi and had the driver take him back down into town. It made sense, he thought. If they were going to go, then they would go now. There was no aircraft carrier in port now, nor was there any large ship due in. So, there was no money to be made right now. The girls had taken the chance, the opportunity, for a vacation. But this is at my expense, he thought. At my expense. Rosie would have known I was coming today. She had to know, unless she was a fool, and she is no fool. So maybe she doesn't care anymore. That follows logically. She doesn't care if I wait around wondering what the fuck for a day or two days or three. And even if she does still care then maybe she doesn't want me to know. But it wouldn't make much sense if she cared, that she wouldn't want me to know. Shit! I don't know what to think. Maybe it does make sense for her. To her. Well, when she returns and I see her again she will have to tell me that she cares. Because I won't do anything until then.

Maybe she doubts me. Maybe she doesn't really believe that I love her. I don't really believe it myself, anyway. Not completely. How could anyone love a whore? A real whore, a prostitute that takes money, demands money, for her body. For the use of her body. And not a slut or even a cheap whore either. She is an *expensive one*. The least you could have done was fall in love, if you had to fall in love at all, with a *cheap* whore. But that way of thinking doesn't make any sense either. She has not ever asked for money. Not once, not either of the two times you have actually made love with her, not that first time that she asked you to come home with her, nor the fantastic time in the hotel in the afternoon at White Rock beach. So, what does any of that mean? What does Rosie mean to you? And what do you mean to her?

"Stop here," Paul told the driver of the cab, and the driver stopped and Paul got out in the rain and let it make him wet, not bothering with the umbrella at all, while he argued with the driver over the amount of the change he had received. The driver went away mad, cursing station sailors, and Paul went through the rain and into Ding's.

It was quiet inside, dark and cool and Don Frank was there. In his corner with his cherry brandy and his long face, thought Paul. I don't really know why I am suddenly so moody. So gloomy.

He went and got a glass of ice from the bar and joined Frank and his bottle.

"Why didn't you get some Seven-Up?" Frank asked.

Paul said nothing and went back to the bar and got two bottles of Seven-Up from the Filipina who sat knitting a sweater behind the bar. He went back to the table and sat down again.

"Rosie wasn't home?" asked Frank.

"Nope."

They mixed the Seven-Up and the cherry brandy half and half and stirred the ice in it with their fingers and began to drink. They sipped the pink liquid slowly, and after a few sips Paul lit his second cigarette of the day.

"May I have one?" said Frank.

"No."

"Give me the cherry brandy back then."

"Give me the Seven-Up back."

"Fine. I'll drink the cherry brandy and you can get drunk on the Seven-Up." Frank grinned.

"I'll give you a cigarette but let me tell you you're starting to remind me of a *Joe*, always asking for a cigarette like that."

"No, the Joe's always ask for one stick. 'One stick cigarette, hey buddy.' Like that."

"None of them is my buddy. I never give them a cigarette and I never smile at them," said Paul.

"Roli," said. Frank. "I've seen you give him all kinds of cigarettes, legal and otherwise. And Rusty. And George." They were the Freedom Highway band.

"Those aren't Joe's. Those are people. Pot heads too, I'll admit."

"I still wouldn't give them my wallet to hold for me while I fought somebody," said Frank.

"I wouldn't either," said Paul. Then he said, "Rosie and Margaret have gone to Manila."

"Oh. When will they be back?"

"I don't know. They didn't tell me. The Mama-san didn't know. Nobody knows but them and I doubt if they know themselves. Besides with this rain the highway will wash out and they'll be stuck there."

"Fucking Joe roads," said Frank.

"Fucking Joe country," said Paul. He took a big drink now, having gotten used to the sweetness made it easier for him to take a big drink. It glowed, rather than burned, its way down. It made a center of warmth in his stomach.

"Where is Linda?" he asked.

"I don't know," said Frank.

"Are you guys in another fight again?"

"No," said Don Frank. "But I don't really give a fuck if I see her today."

"No?"

"No."

"Then what will we do today?"

"I don't know. Get drunk."

"Should we go to Carmen's and buy a matchbox and smoke it all? Or should we go out to Papagayos and eat a Mexican dinner in the morning? It's still morning and it feels like the afternoon. It's this fucking rain. Maybe we should go back to the base or to a hotel and just sleep all day?"

"I don't know," said Don Frank.

"This cherry brandy does not taste so good to me today," said Paul.

"To me either," said Frank.

"Then what?" said Paul. "What should we do today?"

"I know," said Frank.

"What? Tell me your great idea."

"If you put it that way I don't want to tell you," said Don Frank.

"I don't want to go get another rubdown or a steam bath, if that's your idea."

"It's not."

"Then what?"

"It's a dumb idea. You wouldn't want to."

"How do you know what I would or wouldn't want to do? I've done a lot of things in this town that you don't know about."

"Then maybe you'll have already done this."

"Tell me what it is then."

"No."

"Tell me."

"Have you ever heard of the East End Club?" asked Don Frank.

"That's the one way out at the end of the town?"

"Yes."

"I've never been there."

"Neither have I."

"Then let's go," said Paul. "We've nothing to lose."

They took a taxi from Ding's and told the driver where they wanted to go. The driver went up Magsaysay and turned right on Rizal and drove out the muddy street until he came to the traffic circle where he veered off on a side street that ran almost parallel with Rizal. At the next big intersection, he came to a stop. The East End Club was on the opposite corner upstairs and it was the only club around.

There were several girls inside the club, sitting in pairs or groups of three at different tables. There were no customers in the club. The jukebox played a Johnny Cash song. Paul and Frank ignored the looks of the hostess girls and went to the bar where they ordered beers. They sat down then, at a table in the back of the club against the wall. It was dark in the club, and still raining outside.

"This place is dead," said Paul. He sipped his bear.

"It's cool in here man. Something will happen," said Don Frank.

"And this beer is too warm," said Paul.

"Those two girls over there. See, they're looking over here," said Frank. "Look at them."

"I see them," said Paul. He lit another cigarette. He felt grumpy.

"They're not too bad looking," said Frank.

"I guess. Okay, they're not bad at all," said Paul. He looked at the two girls.

They might as well have been twins. They both were young looking, sixteen or so at the oldest he guessed. They both had the light skin color of the Chinese, and they both had long straight black hair. The one girl had slightly thicker, wavier looking hair. She was the better looking of the two girls, he decided. Paul decided to let Frank have that one.

"Call them over here if you want," he said. "You can have the one in the pink. I'll take the thinner one in the brown."

"What if I don't want the one in the pink?" asked Frank.

"She's the better looking one. She even has the best legs. Besides I don't care which one you want, I want the one in the brown."

"Maybe I don't want either one of them," said Frank, grinning.

"I do you a favor and you argue with me. Call them over here." Fuck Rosie, he thought. Fuck this hot gloomy rainy day and fuck her for leaving me without telling me anything. He sucked on the warm beer.

Frank waved at the girls to come the next time he caught them looking. They looked at each other and the one in the brown said something to the one in the pink. Then the one in the pink got up and came over to where Paul and Frank were sitting.

"Did you want to ask me something?" she asked. She was not as young as Paul had guessed, maybe nineteen or twenty, he thought.

"My name is Paul, and this is Don. He would like you to sit with him. What is wrong with your friend?"

"We do not work here and the manager will get mad if we sit with a customer."

"You don't work here?" asked Don Frank.

"My name is Rosie," she said. "I am a go-go dancer here. Not a hostess."

"Rosie huh?" said Paul. He smiled at Frank. "What is your friend's name?"

"Raquel. She dances here too. We are not *hostess girls*."

"We'll meet you outside," said Paul.

Rosie smiled and went back to the table where her friend sat watching. After some conversation she came back and said, "My friend would like to go very much. Wait for us outside."

"We'll just finish our beers," said Paul.

"We will wait," said the little Rosie, and she went back to her seat.

"For future reference," said Frank, "we will call this one Rosie number two."

Paul smiled then. "Who," he asked, "is Rosie number one?"

"Your Rosie," said Frank.

"She is not *my Rosie*. She is Rosie's Rosie. Queen of Olongapo."

Now it was night and Paul lay in the bed that was too soft with the girl Raquel in her room of the house that she and the little Rosie shared. In the other room Paul could hear Frank and Rosie laughing. The girl was warm next to him as he lay in the dark on his back and her head with its soft long hair was on his shoulder. She was asleep and the weight of her head did not bother him and he could feel and hear her breathing, low and regular. It had always surprised him how much these people slept and also the way they slept. They slept very peacefully and they were hard to wake. He thought that Rosie, his Rosie as Frank had called her, was at her best in the morning when she woke. He had been there enough times in the morning waiting for her to wake up, he thought. But certainly not enough times in the bed with her. No, there was only the one time that he'd awakened with her in the morning, and that had been the time that they'd gone bar-hopping together and she'd asked him to come home with her and he'd been surprised and very happy. But there was only that one time of waking with her and only the one other time of love-making.

Now as he lay there with the girl Raquel he thought that probably there wouldn't be any more times with Rosie at all. No, he thought, not now. Not after this with Raquel. The girl Raquel was something, all right. And young. Much younger than Rosie, much younger than the four years difference in their age, he thought. Raquel is not spoiled yet, he thought. And she likes sex much more than Rose does. Rose or Rosie, the same in the end. But Raquel. Certainly not as beautiful, he thought. No, certainly not. But much better. God, in bed much better. Anyway, Rosie won't care. She doubtless won't care.

There was a loud knock at the door and then Frank's voice said, "Hey Sutton!"

"Yes." Paul lay there on the bed nude with the girl Raquel knowing there was no lock on the door and hoping Frank would not open it.

"You okay?"

"Yeah."

"We're going now."

"Okay. Bye then," said Paul.

"You going to stay here? Rosie has to go to work."

The girl had awakened and had listened and now Paul saw that she was smiling and nodding her head. "Yes," said Paul. "We are going to stay."

There was a silence. Then, "Okay buddy. See ya later."

"Alright," said Paul.

Together they heard the door close as they lay there and then the girl giggled. She leaned over and kissed Paul on the mouth. He smiled happily at her. In a low voice, her face now serious, she said, "Give me your tongue."

They kissed again and explored each other's mouths with their tongues, Paul working softly and the girl Raquel, hungrily. Her hands explored his body and excited him and it was not long before she had mounted him and together, almost instantly, they came. For Paul it was the whole world moving and rocking and only himself and the girl were steady, locked together un-moving while the world was a chaos around them.

And afterwards the girl said, "Always together. Four times now and each time together. Why is that?"

They lay there together and Paul said, "I don't know. I've never known such a thing before."

"Do you have a girl in the States?" asked Raquel.

"Yes," said Paul. "A girlfriend. Not a wife."

"You butterfly?" said the girl. "How come you butterfly?"

"Not a butterfly," said Paul. "She is eight thousand miles away, and I'm here."

"You butterfly," said the girl. "And how about here? You got girlfriend here?"

"No.".

"Don't lie! You said before that you've been here fifteen months now."

"I had a girlfriend," said Paul. "But now there is only you."

The girl laughed. "You bullshit me," she said laughing.

"If you want to be my girl," said Paul.

Raquel put her head down on his chest. He could feel her lips moving on him. "I want," she said. Then she looked up at him. "I think I want your baby too," she said, laughing again.

CHAPTER 16

Paul sat at a table in Kong's restaurant with the girl Raquel drinking a Cuba Libre and smoking a cigarette. He was smiling at the girl and he was very happy.

Raquel was not looking at him, instead she played with her hands nervously, every now and then clearing her throat softly.

Paul smiled happily at her and said, "Two days. Two days! I'm so short that it takes me an hour to cross a crack in the sidewalk."

The girl looked at him. "Do not joke," she said.

Paul's manner changed. "I'm sorry," he said.

"You come and then you go," said the girl.

"I know," said Paul.

It was almost noon and outside it was sunny and warm and Paul was thinking now that it was over. The PI was over. It was his next to last day in the Philippines and he was going back to *the world* and he was going to get out of the Navy. It did not seem real to him now, but it was beginning to feel more real since yesterday when he and Don Frank had finished checking out. And it was beginning to seem more real as he watched the girl trying to maintain herself. He was only now becoming aware of this.

"Raquel," he said.

The girl looked at him. Her black eyes were very open and her lips parted slightly to show her very perfect small white teeth and her face seemed very calm. But her hands still worked nervously with one another.

"Raquel," he said again. "I have cared more for you than any other girl I have known here. Or any girl anywhere. I am glad to be going home but I don't like leaving you. I wanted to tell you how I feel about you, and I hope you believe me."

She smiled happily, the smile that Paul had come to look for and that he always wanted from her. It was the smile that made her seem innocent like a child, it was the smile that made him feel as if he'd pleased her. And she showed him this smile now. It was only there for a few seconds but it made him feel less guilty about his own happiness.

She said, "Tonight, we..." and she giggled. Then she laughed openly.

"Tonight," said Paul.

"I want you tonight," said the girl, her face now flat and looking very Chinese. "Tonight, you give me baby to remember you. Souvenir," she said, laughing again.

Paul laughed too. "No," he said, smiling at her joke.

The girl looked at the watch she wore. It was a large silver man's watch with a metal band and her wrist was too small for it. She looked at it and said, "I have to go to work."

"I'll see you tonight," said Paul. "I'll be there before closing."

The girl Raquel smiled and stood up and thanked him for her lunch. She leaned over and kissed him close to his ear quickly, and then she left.

Paul watched her get into a Jeepney outside through the window. He sighed. Well, he thought, I cannot help it any. I have to go home and that's all there is for her. But he could not contain his happiness. It welled up inside of him, from somewhere unknown, brought on by the thought of going home, of really going home and getting out of the Navy.

I wonder what Mary will be like now, he thought, after knowing these girls here. It has been said somewhere that all women are really just whores and that is certainly true here. Almost literally true, he thought. No, don't go philosophizing, he told himself. Many of these women became whores out of necessity. And the opportunity made by the stupid war. But so what? Mary is not a whore, neither out of desire or necessity or even by her nature. She is a white Anglo-Saxon American girl with blond hair and blue eyes and she has to shave her legs twice a week. Raquel is not any of these things and she is a *not* a whore. And she has only been a dancer since her eighteenth birthday which was only nine months ago, or so she says anyway. Well, so what? It doesn't make her any better or worse than Mary or Rosie or anyone here for that matter. Don't think of what is going to happen to her now that you're going. The only difference in your going home is that you won't be here to watch it happen to her. Why think of it now? Let it alone. Just think about going home.

A wave of happiness hit him again and he let it roll over him and get into him. He stubbed out his cigarette and lit another and drank some more of his Cuba Libre. He wondered where Don Frank was. He was supposed to be here an hour ago. I have spent more time waiting for him since I have been here than the number of cigarettes I have smoked, he thought, giving one hour to each cigarette. Always he is late or forgets to come entirely.

Well, *so what* of that too. Big deal. Just think about going home and all the problems are left behind. Can you believe it! No, I can't believe it. Exactly eighteen months I've been here, or almost exactly anyway. Now I'm going home and I'm a *short-timer* and it's time to say goodbye to everybody here and wish them luck. I'll have to go into the New Life club and say goodbye to Roli and his brothers tonight. And to see Rosie and Mar. Well, Margaret anyway, he thought. Rosie will not care that I'm leaving. She might care. Who knows? I'm not sure that she won't care, because I'm not sure whether she cares about me and Raquel. Couldn't tell by the way she acted, he thought.

He thought of the first night that he had seen Rosie again. It was really the first night he had seen her since the time Don Frank had talked to her. It was the first time since he'd met Raquel. Both she and her sister had changed jobs and were now working at the New Life Club. It was late and he had gone alone to the New Life to hear the music and when he had come in the door Rosie had been standing just inside. He looked at her but she did not look at him, so he had walked on going towards the dance floor with the intention of crossing it and finding an empty table. The Freedom Highway was playing a very slow blues number and it was only as he had reached the middle of the dance floor that he became aware of Rosie walking at his side. He stopped and looked at her and she looked at him. She said nothing but took his arm instead and put it around her waist and folded herself against him and then they were dancing. Paul could think of no words and he held her close to him, feeling her nails on his back through his shirt. He had danced this way with her before and always it was something. Now he could think of nothing to say, his mind racing between Raquel and his doubts and what was happening just now. Rosie could make you feel like God when she danced that way with you. And the thought that was racing in his mind with all the other thoughts was that yeah, but she danced that way with everybody, when it was a slow dance. He reached for that thought as he danced with her there on the dance floor of the New Life club that night, trying to hold on to it.

And then when the dance had ended she had led him to a table and had gone and gotten him a coke, which was all he wanted ever right then, and she had sat down and looked at him haughtily and said, "After the band is through we will talk."

So, they had sat there waiting, Paul's mind still racing between the girl Raquel and this girl-woman who sat next to him now with all her power over him, power that he could feel but did not know how to resist. They sat and waited and he tried to calm himself by chain smoking.

Then when the music was over she said, "You." Her voice was as low as he'd ever heard it. "You, you, you," she said, her eyes unreadable in the dim lighting of the club.

"Yes," he said.

"I hope you are very happy with your new girlfriend", she said.

"She is not my girlfriend." And he felt that there was never a truer thing than that at that moment. But even as he said it there was guilt in his gut.

"Oh no?" she said. "Yes, I think so. For you and me it is over anyway. You know that. It is better."

"It's only over," Paul said slowly, "because you wanted it that way."

"It is over because of you," she said, and looked away.

"No. I have told you. So many times."

Rosie turned on him angrily.

"Always you speak of this *love*," she said. "Love, love, love! What is this love you speak of? I don't see it. Not on you. As soon as I go to Manila, you go find this girl. Maybe you love her too?"

"Every time I told you, I meant it. Like I told you," said Paul. "And I see now that it would have been better maybe to just treat you like a whore, or just a bitch."

Rosie shrugged. "It doesn't matter," she said. "I have too many boyfriends already." She looked at him and spoke then with quiet earnestness. "Anyway, it is better. Sure, I *like* you. But I don't feel this love you always talk of. This is not the place for that. So, I say okay, be my *station boyfriend*, and I will be very good to you. But my profession, it is in the way of this love of yours, so it is better."

Now thinking of that night as he sat in Kong's restaurant, he could not keep from being angry. To think of lowering himself like that! He was glad that he was going home, because of that. What had he been thinking of? Oh, she'd had him by the balls alright. A woman like that, that looked and moved and smelled and had that voice of hers, she could get any guy hooked that way. Sure. That's why they're called hookers. What angered him most was that she'd probably done it on purpose. Well, I'm going home, he thought.

Just then Rosie walked in with her sister Margaret and a tall sailor in whites who was obviously off of a ship and also obviously with Margaret, and not with Rosie. Rosie wore an orange jump suit, her hair hanging in a heavy pony-tail and she was relaxing. Margaret was obviously not relaxing but doing business with the sailor in his whites. Paul grinned when they waved at him from their table. It was Mar who was really doing the waving. Rosie was studying the menu and besides she had her back to him. Margaret called for Paul to join them.

Well, what the hell, thought Paul. I will tell them goodbye and make the sailor in whites feel bad. He went over and sat with them. It was a square table and the sailor, who was a second-class Petty Officer and therefore maybe a lifer, sat opposite him. Rosie was on his left, still studying her menu, and Margaret on his right.

He spoke to Margaret, saying, "Well, I guess I should say good-bye. I'm leaving tomorrow."

"Tomorrow!" said Margaret.

"Well, we go to Clark Air Force Base tomorrow, but we don't get a plane 'til the next day." He smiled at the sailor across the table from him. "Getting out," he said.

The sailor smiled indulgently. "Going back to *the World*, huh?"

"Yep, I've been here over eighteen months now, and it's time to go home."

"That's really neat!" said the sailor. "Good for you!"

"And your friend?" said Margaret.

"Don Frank? He's going home too. Together as always," he smiled.

"Oh," said Margaret. "I liked him very much, but I don't think he liked me."

"Sure he did," said Paul.

Rosie snorted. But she did not look up from her menu. Her face and eyes were bare, and clean of any visible make-up.

Margaret said, "And your new girlfriend? Raquel? Is she unhappy?"

"Well, I don't know," said Paul.

"Oh yes, you know," said Margaret, "and if you were my boyfriend you would be taking me home with you!" She ignored Paul's' laugh and went on, "Sure. Or my sister too. We both know how to please a man very good. Better than Raquel, who is only a child."

The sailor looked uncomfortable. Paul knew she was joking from the expression on her face. Perversely he said, "I don't know about that. That girl is the best sex I've ever had, anytime or anywhere."

"Better than my sister?"

"Okay, no. Maybe not. Well, just different," said Paul seriously. He glanced at Rosie. She had looked up quickly at her sister and then back down at her menu. She was biting her lower lip and Paul could see that her eyes were moving quickly back and forth across the menu.

"But maybe that was because she likes it." He felt immediately bad.

"Humph," snorted Rosie.

"Bullshit," said Margaret. "My sister and I are much experienced. Maybe it is true that we do not enjoy it always. But what do you expect? Maybe we get tired of it."

The sailor was looking at her with an expression of amusement.

"Okay, I can understand that," said Paul.

"Your girlfriend, soon she will get tired too."

"She is not *formally* my girlfriend, you know. We just have some fun together."

"And you could not have fun with my sister?"

Paul shrugged. He did not look at Rosie, and he did not look at the sailor.

"Well, you should have tried me, then," said Margaret, making it into a joke again.

Paul said, grinning, "I didn't know you were available."

"Anytime," said Margaret, laughing.

Paul looked at Rosie. She was still looking at her menu. "You," he said. "You, Rosie. Why don't you say something?"

"Why don't you go find your girl," said Rosie without looking up.

That made the sailor laugh.

Paul looked at him and shook his head sorrowfully. "Well, good luck buddy," he said, and then he got up from the table and walked out of the New Life Club forever and went out to the East End Club where the girl Raquel worked. It was his last day in town.

PART THREE

THE OLD MAN IN THE

RESTAURANT

(1973)

CHAPTER 17

Thereherehere would be five hours of flying time before they reached Manila. As soon as he saw the No Smoking light go out Paul loosened his seat belt and brought his seat back to a position that allowed him to see out of the window easily. Below there was the big blue ocean, very blue in the early morning light. They were still climbing and just at that moment they entered a cloud so that all Paul could see was the wing. Then they were out of it again and the plane banked left and the sun was in Paul's face. He pulled down the plastic curtain and lit a cigarette.

There is nothing like flying in a big jet, he thought, except when you think about what would happen if they lost power in all four engines. Gliding five feet forward for every five thousand feet of falling. Or something like that. But it' s better not to think about those kinds of things when you're in the air. Or even when you're waiting at the airport and getting ready for the flight. Or any time, for that matter.

But if it happens, it happens, he thought. Worry about it when it happens. What I need is another drink. Certainly, a drink. Look at that, he said to himself. Getting back into it already aren't you? Getting back into the drinking. Oh, you're ready for the PI alright. Ha ha! Am I really? Oh yes I am. Or at least I will be when I get there. Well, I don't have to worry about it right now then, do I? Okay, no you don't. Maybe I won't even stay. Maybe. I've got five hours to decide about it. Certainly. Five hours at 30,000 feet and fifty cents a drink. Great.

The stewardess came down the aisle with her drink tray and Paul ordered a scotch sour.

"No, I don't want the breakfast," he told her. "I had my breakfast at the hotel in Tokyo."

It was amazing that they had such drinks as scotch sours on the planes. They certainly didn't have them when you were flying in the States, he thought. No, they didn't. Scotch and soda yes. Martinis already mixed, yes. Scotch sours no. Cuba Libre's no. It was amazing too because in the States it was a dollar a drink on the planes. And here they mixed them for you. It is so nice to fly, he thought. He felt contented.

The drink tasted very good and it warmed him and took away the slight tightness in his stomach. He put on his sunglasses and then he raised the plastic curtain of the window again and looked out.

It was so beautiful. It really is, he thought. That's a word that's not used much anymore. Beautiful. Tokyo was beautiful. Someday I should go there when I have more time than one night in a hotel and really see it. Sure, really see it. No, I mean it. I'd know where to go alright. Certainly, I'd know where to go. After the Philippines you learn about Asia, or that is you've learned about Asia enough to get you through any of the countries here. You think so? Yes. Yes, because you'd go where the poor people were and where the slums are and where the whores are and where the sailors were because you love that and it would be the same. Or enough like it to seem the same and you'd know how to take care of yourself. Certainly, I'd know how to take care of myself. But I don't like that part about loving it. I'm not sure I really like that part at all. Then why did you say it? I don't know. You do know that that is where you'd always go? Yes, I know it. Then why do you think that is? You might as well admit it. Okay, so, I admit it. Maybe. Yes, you admit it. There is no maybe. You admit it because it's true and the reason for it is true, and also the reason you don't want to admit it is true. It is because of Rosie. She is part of it and it is because of finding her like a flower in all the ugliness that you love it.

I am not going to admit that right now, he thought. Although I'm thinking it, I'm not admitting it. Although I have to admit that I want to see her and can't wait to see her, I won't admit it right now because I am afraid to see her. And also, because I know I only want to see her because of *that dream*. I never should have told Don Frank about that dream. Fool that I am. Anyway, it isn't because of the past and what really happened that I want to see her. It is only because of the fantasy of that dream. What a dream.

Well, I just won't think about that dream. Not anymore. Better to think about what I'm going to do when I get there. Shit, I'm only supposed to be going to Australia.

The stewardess came by again with her tray and Paul ordered another scotch sour and asked what time they would arrive in Manila.

"Ten-forty Manila time," she told him.

She returned with his drink and gave him his change from his five-dollar bill.

"Will you be going on with us to Sidney?" she asked. She was a pretty Japanese girl and she spoke perfect English, with no accent that he could detect.

"I don't know," said Paul. "My ticket is good for Sidney, but I might stay a few days in Manila."

"It's the middle of their rainy season," she told him. "It's very bad."

"Oh, it's almost over. September isn't too bad. I was stationed there in the service, you see. Navy."

"Oh," she said. "Well, there's a typhoon moving in that area, you know. Might get to the Philippines pretty soon. Of course, it might not. Anyway, I hope you have a nice stay there." She smiled at him and moved away with her tray.

Well, I haven't decided yet, thought Paul. I'm very glad this plane is so empty, though. He had three seats to himself and now he folded the armrests up and put his legs up in the seat next to him, sitting with his back to the window, feeling the imagined warmth of the sun. He sipped his drink slowly.

To be perfectly honest, he thought, there is really only one reason I want to go back to Olongapo. Only one reason. Does it hurt to be honest? I don't know. But I must be honest because I already know it's true. Not being honest wouldn't make it any less true. No, I have to be honest. There is really only one reason for wanting to go back there or for thinking about going back there and it isn't curiosity or nostalgia. It is because of her. Certainly.

To be honest it is because of her. There was something with us. There must have been something. I have never dreamed about any girl before. Or woman. I don't think of her as a girl, I think of her as a woman. Bullshit, a girl. That's what she would say. She calls herself and thinks of herself as a woman. So, you romanticize and tell yourself that you think of her that way also. Don't romanticize her. That is a mistake. Think of her clearly, as you would think of any other. Like you thought of Mary. Maybe that is what Rosie meant for you to do when she argued with you about love. Well, I don't know. She was impossible to understand. So, you fall in love for the first time and you have to do it with a whore. A prostitute, not a whore. Don't degrade her either. Don't romanticize her and don't degrade her. Well, I'm sorry. But there is only a very fine line between a whore and a prostitute. Certainly, it is very hard for me to see the difference but it is truly there or else there wouldn't be so many sailors marrying them and bringing them back to the States. They could see the difference and I'm pretty sure Rosie is not a goddamn whore. Maybe that's what I should have done too.

One thing I am sure of though is that she is a difficult person. Too stubborn and too proud and too sure of every damn thing. Very difficult. A prostitute out of necessity and maybe greed, OK. Well, I don't know about the greed, but I do know about the *necessity*. In that respect she was just like every other woman in that town. If the country were not so poor and the government not so damn corrupted she would not be so poor or corrupted either. You're romanticizing again. No, I am not. It's true about the necessity, but what is also true is that if things had been different in the PI she would have found and married the richest farmer or banker she could. Of course, and she has lost that chance forever. If she ever had it.

But it's also true that if it were not for the war and the necessity it made I would never have met her. So I guess I had better go find her. Yes, why not? To be completely honest it is the only thing I can do. It's probably too late for us, but it's still the right thing to do. He smiled at himself and began to think of how he was going to get from Manila to Olongapo safely.

CHAPTER 18

The plane landed at Manila International Airport on time and under typical blue and white cloud tropical sky. It wasn't raining but the old familiar moist tropical heat hit Paul as he stepped off the plane onto the ramp and this heat brought the four drinks he had consumed right up into his head.

Customs was the worst thing, as he knew it would be. They wanted to know how much money he had, how long he was going to stay, whether he had been here before, and most of all they wanted an address.

"I'm going to Olongapo City," Paul told the official in the hot looking starched khaki uniform.

"But why do you wish to go there?"

"I already told you. I was there before, when I was in the Navy."

"Yes?"

"I just want to go see some old friends there."

"Filipino or American?"

"Both," lied Paul. He sighed.

"And what will your address be there?"

"The Newport Hotel," said Paul. It was the only one he could remember, just then.

"Do you have a reservation there?" asked the official, writing in his little book.

"No. You don't need reservations there, they always have empty rooms."

"Are you sure of this?"

"Yes."

"Do you know the address of this hotel?"

"No. I mean, not exactly. It's on Magsaysay Avenue, close to the American Legion."

"And how much money will you carry there?"

"Enough," said Paul. His old wariness was back.

"Please, I need to know the exact amount."

"About three hundred dollars' worth of Pesos," Paul told him, sighing again. "I'm going to leave the rest of my traveler's checks at the bank here in Manila."

"You must be very careful of your money in this country," said the official, smiling for the first time.

"Yes," said Paul.

After Customs and Immigration there came a multitude of brown faces and warm bodies that Paul would have to pass through to get outside. And there were all the taxi drivers and airport porters and as he pushed through the crowd it seemed that every one of them wanted to carry his single black bag for him. He crossed through the crowd holding his bag tightly with one hand while keeping the other hand in his front pocket where he had put his wallet.

Halfway through the crowd he saw that there was a branch office of the Central Bank at the airport, and he headed for this, which required a change of direction.

He had four thousand dollars in travelers checks and two hundred and fifty-three dollars in cash and he changed two twenty dollar checks and all of his cash for Pesos. The rate here was 7.3 Pesos to one American dollar. So, he had over 2100 Pesos. It was good enough. He deposited the rest of his traveler's checks with the bank for safety and went outside to see about a taxi.

"Hey Joe, you want taxi? Here, here."

Paul walked along the front of the terminal slowly. Many were calling out to him as he passed, offering rides in their cabs, but he was undecided. He suddenly trusted none of the people that he did not personally know in this country, and he knew none of them here. He stopped. Now there is something, he said to himself. He began to smile.

Across the street there was a parking lot and in it now there was a blue Chevrolet. Paul recognized the color. It was a Navy Special Services car and right now there was an officer in his whites getting out of it and the driver, a Filipino, was opening the trunk and getting bags out of it. Then the driver shut the trunk and stood smiling. One of the airport porters came over and started helping the officer get his baggage on a cart and across the street towards the terminal. The driver stood smiling, watching them go.

That Filipino driver, thought Paul, wasn't about to save that officer his tip, but he's about to help me get to Subic. Whether it's against the rules or not.

Paul crossed the street and went over to the driver, who was about to get back into the car, and smiling he called out, "Hey, hold on for a sec buddy!"

The driver stopped and at looked back at Paul. He was a short man, even for his race, and he had to look up at Paul. He was very brown and chubby and he wore an old golf style shirt and baggy khaki pants that were too long, but his shoes were new looking brown loafers. He smiled up at Paul.

Paul smiled back even more warmly. "Want a cigarette?" he asked.

The driver nodded and took one and stuck it behind his ear.

"Have another," said Paul.

This time the driver lit the cigarette. He looked curiously at Paul.

"Sorry, they're not menthol," Paul told him.

"That's okay," said the driver. "You Navy?"

"No," said Paul. "Not anymore." He smiled.

"Where you go?"

"I want to go to Olongapo City. I figure you're going to Subic, right?"

The driver smiled. "Maybe you get married?" He laughed.

"No," said Paul.

"Maybe you give me fifty dollars?"

"I'll give you twenty Pesos," said Paul.

The driver nodded. "I think you used to be in Navy here. Station maybe, huh?"

"Yeah, at Cubi. So, let's go. Twenty Pesos."

The driver shrugged, grinning. "Fifty pesos."

It was a long ride. Going through Manila he thought it was like a joke because he had heard so much about it and now he saw that the city was almost like a false front. Like a western movie set. Behind many of the big buildings and hotels and fancy new art palaces and community centers there were the same old slums.

Then they were out of the city on the new highway, which Paul had to pay the toll fee for because the driver wouldn't, and they were passing Victory Liners and old beat up trucks carrying what looked like old trash back in the States and making good time. It still wasn't raining, but out towards the South China Sea Paul could see the heavy dark clouds.

The countryside was the same. He hadn't expected it to change, but he was still somehow unprepared for the sheer beauty of it. It had always surprised him before, and it did now. Out in the country away from the slum cities and the dirty little towns and barrios it was clean. So clean and so green and so alive. They were passing through the flatland's, through the cornfields and barley fields and rice paddies north and west of Manila, with the green mountains always framing everything. Along the highway they passed farmers riding Caribou carts, lots of Jeepneys even out here, and the tiny Filipino horses pulling plows in the red earth, and everything seemed so very green and fresh, and somehow also very old and timeless, and after so much time away from here, it felt like a great and pleasant surprise to him.

The driver did not talk much, but like every Filipino Paul had ever ridden with here, he drove hard and fast and even a little dangerously, but casually at the same time.

It is something to be back, thought Paul. I will ignore this guy's driving and think of that. It is *really something* to be back. None of it looks any different than before. But it all looks new too!

Well, why should it look different? Hell, I don't know why I feel so happy right now. Damn, if it looks any different! And it seems somehow new. Well, when I get to town I will go straight into Kong's and drink my first San Miguel. No, I will go to Ding's. Damn if I know what I will do. Rosie might be in Kong's. Yeah, so? You've come here to see her, haven't you? Yes. No. Yes and no at once. But I have to see her, now that I'm really here. That's for sure. It doesn't make any difference exactly what I was thinking before. Now that I'm here, I have to find Rosie. *Fucking A!*

He could see now that they were coming closer to San Fernando, where the road from Angeles City and Clark Air Force Base joined the road from Manila on its way to Subic Bay, and from there made its way on up the coast to the Lingayen Gulf. They were halfway home.

CHAPTER 19

You remember me," said Paul.

"Of course, I remember! What you think? That I'm going to forget? We remember every man that we ever meet," Mar said happily.

"Well thanks, I'm glad you do. Mainly I'm also very glad that you still live here. In the same house. I was worried about that."

"Yes, you are lucky. Rosie and me, we will move soon. Go back to Manila. We are sick of this town."

Paul sat on one of the quilt covered soft beds that took up the entire wall of one end of the room. Everything was exactly the same as he remembered it.

Margaret sat next to him on the edge of the bed and looked at him. "Your hair is very long now," she said. "It looks very good. Rosie will like it, I think. But I don't know what she will say about that beard."

"Rosie," said Paul.

"You are the first one that ever came back," said Margaret. "Why you come back to this place for?"

"I'm going to Australia," said Paul.

"Why?"

"For surfing. I don't know. It's too cold in California."

"Too cold?"

"For me, yes."

"Ha! You are a Filipino now, huh? You don't like to be so cold anymore."

Paul laughed a little.

"Rosie is in Manila. To see our Mother. I'm angry with her now. Rosie. Three days she has been gone. And the rent is due tomorrow." She looked at Paul sadly. "She is very, how you say it? Forgetting things all the time?"

"Forgetful?" said Paul. "Absentminded?"

"Yes, absentminded. All the time she is forgetting things now. See, she had duty yesterday at the club. Because she didn't come home, last night, the manager ask me, 'Where is Rosie? How come she didn't come today?' I say she is in Manila. I tell him our mama is sick, but he say that he is getting tired of Rosie. Always taking time off. And he say she never sits with the customers anymore. That is true, you know. All the time she just sits in the corner by herself. I don't know what the problem with her is. Maybe soon she'll get fired."

Paul looked at Mar and said, "So, she doesn't have a boyfriend now?" His throat felt tight as he asked.

"No no, not for a long time. Neither do I. No boyfriends! Rosie and I decided, from now on, only business. No boyfriends. It's better for us."

"I guess it would be," said Paul.

"Yes. But Rosie will be glad to see you, I think. She has your picture in her wallet, you know."

"She has a lot of pictures in her wallet," said Paul, looking up at a framed picture of Rosie hanging on the wall. She truly was beautiful, he thought.

Mar shrugged and said, "Why you no write to us? Why you come back?"

"I guess you know why."

"Maybe you come to see Raquel?"

"No."

"Rosie will think that."

"I'm not going to try to see Raquel," said Paul.

"Anyway, I heard Raquel got married."

Paul shrugged.

"She moved to Chicago with her Fleetie husband."

"Good for her."

"I will help you with her," Mar told him. "But it's hard to understand Rosie. I am her sister. We live together! And I don't understand her. Nobody but Rosie understands Rosie very much. You remember. You know her. But for someone to come back...that has never happened before! I think she will be very happy."

"I'll see you tonight," said Paul.

"Yes, I have to get ready for work now. It' s late."

Paul went to Kong' s and sat in the back room, the green room, where it was air-conditioned. It was late in the afternoon after talking with Margaret and the back room was nearly empty. There were two older men who sat together in the corner window talking and a young Marine who sat alone by the wall close to the open doorway that led into the front dining room. The two in the corner looked to be Officers, thought Paul. Like Navy or Marine Officers wearing civvies. And that Marine corporal. Waiting for a girl, I'll bet. A girl who is late.

Paul sat at a small table in the center of the room on one of the little chairs that made you feel like a midget, and he sat so that he could see both the Marine near the doorway and the two Officers in the corner opposite the Marine. He did not like to sit with his back to people. Yes, it was all coming back now, like he'd hardly been gone.

A waitress came through the door by the Marine and walked over towards Paul. She was very pretty in her gray and white uniform. She had a very clean face with no visible make-up at all and pale skin and her hair was very long, reaching to her buttocks. The only thing wrong with her that Paul could see was her legs. He thought they were a bit too thick.

"One San Miguel beer," said Paul. "Philippines, not Manila, and very cold please."

The waitress smiled prettily and went back through the door into the front where the bar was. Paul looked at the Marine who he had found was watching him and the Marine looked back down into his beer glass.

In a minute the waitress came back with a beer and a glass. She put them down on the table in front of Paul, placing the glass first and then the beer bottle upside down in the glass. The beer ran out of the bottle into the glass until it had risen to where the neck of the bottle was, and then it stopped.

"Thank you," said Paul, and he gave her five Pesos. She smiled at him and turned and left. Paul watched her walk away and thought it was too bad for her that she had such thick legs. Then he thought, well, she's just a waitress.

He lit a cigarette and dragged hard on it until his lungs could feel the smoke and then he put the cigarette in the small square ashtray on the table. He lifted the brown beer bottle slowly out of the glass until the glass was full. He drank down what was left in the bottle before he let the smoke out of his lungs and felt dizzy for a second.

The beer was very cold and hard and tangy and it hit his stomach hard. No other beer in the world has such a taste as this, he thought. It's because they use less water to make it and so it's thicker than other beers. Or so it's said. And maybe it's a little green sometimes.

He picked up his cigarette again and as he did so he saw that the Marine was looking at him. Paul looked at him directly, flashed the peace sign and smiled at him and the Marine looked back down into his beer.

The Marine was thin and hard looking and he had very short hair. He was very clean looking too, and so well shaved that the skin of his face looked new and pink.

He must be waiting for his girlfriend, thought Paul. He's bored and impatient looking, and maybe hurt looking. She must be late already, and from the look of him this has happened before. Probably it's happened a couple of times before and maybe he expected it this time. Well, I'm not sure about his looking hurt. That could be something else, or my imagination. But I think he's getting mad. I've seen this before, and in fact it's happened to me before. Waiting for Rosie. Yeah, that's nothing new in this town.

Paul looked away from the Marine and looked at the two men that were probably Officers that sat at the table in the corner.

They were talking together in low voices and they laughed every now and then as if they were joking about something. Paul thought that they were either Officers or maybe civilians that worked for the government on the base. Engineers maybe, he thought. They were casually dressed, dressed for the heat of the tropics. One of the men, the one that looked the oldest because his hair was thinning and going gray, glanced at Paul and smiled and nodded. Paul smiled back and then looked away.

It was then that the old man came in. He was a short skinny old white man whose back was slightly hunched and bent over, and he wore a white *barong-tagalog* shirt and gray baggy pants and filthy rubber flip-flop shoes on his filthy feet. His white hair was thin, almost gone, and he came in shuffling quickly, his head turned back towards the front door and the bar out front.

"Bring me a beer," he was saying loudly. "Bring me a goddamn beer! And hurry it up, ain't got all day." He stopped at a table that was between Paul and the Marine by the door and he sat down heavily in the chair. He was carrying a brown paper bag that was twisted tightly closed. Paul could see that there was a bottle in the bag. The old man placed this on the chair next to him so that the white table cloth that hung down from the table covered it. He looked at Paul and winked his left eye, grinning as he did so. Then he turned around in his chair towards the doorway and said loudly, "Where the hell is my goddamn beer! You know me and you know I always want a goddamn beer." He turned back around and said to to on one in particular, "Can't ever get no goddamn service in here and I been coming in this fucking place for years."

This same old man, thought Paul. I have seen him before, out on the street for years, going this way and that, and always in those same baggy pants and shower shoes. I wonder who he is. He's an American alright, because of his speech and because of his looks. But he's too old for a serviceman and besides he dresses like a

Joe. Maybe he's like me? Maybe he got out twenty or thirty years ago, and never went back home.

A waitress had brought the old man a beer now, but she wasn't the same waitress that had brought Paul his. This one was thin and shorter and a little ugly. She looked very ugly now as she watched the old man pull a few dirty wrinkled Pesos from his shirt pocket. It was obvious that she did not like the old man, and it was with distaste that she took the money from him and left. Paul thought he could understand her distaste.

The old man had turned in his chair and watched her go back through the door and now he reached down and picked up the bottle that was in the paper bag from where he had hidden it on the chair. It was a clear quart bottle of some brown liquor, likely rum, and he twisted the cap off now and drank from it.

He looked at Paul and grinned at him, winking his left eye again. "I just get the beer to cover up," he said. He held the bottle up. "Want a drink?"

Paul smiled friendly like and said, "No thank you."

The old man shrugged and took another drink out of the bottle and then he put the cap back on and put the bottle back into the bag. He left it out on the table now.

The old man was sitting with his back to the doorway and to the Marine, and because he was so short and hunched and the chairs were so low, all Paul could see were the head and shoulders of him. But Paul could see the doorway, which the old man could not, and he saw a young girl come in the room and stop when she saw the old man. She did not look happy to see him, but just grimaced and walked to his table and sat down by him.

"Where the hell you been?" said the old man.

The girl said something in *Tagalog* in a low voice and looked down at the table.

"Don't talk that shit to me, talk English. I don't wanna hear that shit talk. Where you been all morning? I got the right to know, by God."

The girl again said something in a low voice, but it was so low that Paul could not hear what language she used.

The old man said another obscenity and suddenly slapped her face. She rose from the chair and Paul could see that she was near tears. Her face was all screwed up in fury. She spoke loudly to the old man now, her words coming in a fast spitting torrent and in her own language, and when she was done she spun and left the room almost running.

The old man did not look after her and seemed content to just sit and sip his beer. There was silence in the room, even from the Officers, and Paul looked at them. The older one smiled at Paul and shook his head.

"You dirty old man," said the Marine.

The old man turned in his chair and looked at the Marine. "It ain't none of your business boy," he said after a while, and he turned back around again.

"You fucking dirty old man," said the Marine. He was only a corporal, and Paul could detect no accent to give away his home state.

The old man said without looking at him, "Watch your mouth, boy."

"You should talk," said the Marine. His face was reddening and his voice shook as he tried to keep it even. "You didn't have no right to talk to that girl like that! Or to hit her like that. I oughta bust your head, old man."

"I told you to mind your own damn business, boy," said the old man. He had turned sideways in his chair now so that he wouldn't have to turn his head to look at the Marine. "It ain't nobody's business what I say. I say what I want to who I want and no damn punk boy is gonna tell me different."

"If you weren't so fucking old I'd bust your fucking head."

"Well, I ain't afraid of no boy. I'm sixty-three years old and I ain't afraid of no boy-scout boy."

"I'm not a boy," said the Marine. "And you're not a man, you're an old bastard who needs his head broke. If you wanna step outside I'll break it for you."

"Fuck you, boy," said the old man. He was talking loudly now and there were five or six waitresses standing in the doorway by the Marine. "You ain't nothing but a punk boy and I ain't afraid of you. I ain't afraid of that uniform either."

"You didn't have no right to talk to that girl like that. You shouldn't have hit her like that."

"Why the hell not? You tell me why not. All she was is a whore, so you tell me why not." The old man looked around the room at the two officers and at Paul. Then he looked back at the Marine.

"She was pregnant," said the Marine. "Anybody could see she was pregnant."

"Pregnant my ass," said the old man. He laughed. "She's just a fat little whore, that's all. Just a fat little whore. Listen, I know her. Know all the whores in this town. Every damn one of 'em, and I ought to. Been here twenty-five years nearly. This is *my country*, and don't you go trying to tell me how to behave in it. It's my country now, you hear! If I went to your country I wouldn't go telling you what to do!"

The Marine corporal was silent, staring at the old man. "I thought she was pregnant," he said after a bit.

"Some damn boy comes in here and tells me what to do in my own damn country," said the old man. He was looking at the two Officers in the corner. "How do you like that? You think that's right?"

"Don't ask me," said the older Officer. "I haven't got an opinion."

Paul said nothing.

"I don't think it's right," said the old man. He looked back at the Marine and said, "I ain't afraid to fight you, you know. I'd go outside and fight you right now, except I got this bottle here and I can't leave it."

"Let's drop it," said the Marine. His face was not so red anymore.

"If you want to drop it, then that's fine with me. Except you oughta say you're sorry. This is my damn country now, and no damn boy is gonna tell me what to do anyhow."

"I'm not a boy," said the Marine.

"Well, you ain't no damn man. A man don't go buttin' his head into another man's business. Nobody else butted in."

"Okay. So, I'll say it. I'm sorry. It was a mistake."

"You're damn right it was. She weren't no more pregnant than I am. Just a fat whore, is all."

"Okay," said the Marine. He drank deeply from his own beer now.

"And I can't be leaving a good bottle around just to go outside and fight over some whore," said the old man. He turned back around to Paul and said, "You can see that, can't you? "

Paul grinned and nodded. He heard the two men in the corner chuckling.

"You sure you don't want a drink?"

"No, thank you," said Paul, wondering why the old man had singled him out to talk to now.

"Well, you need another beer then. I'll buy everybody a beer." He turned back around in his chair and told one of the waitresses standing in the doorway to bring five new beers.

The Marine said, "That's okay. I still got this beer here."

"Well, drink it up," the old man told him. "'Cause I'm buying you a beer. Unless you want some of this rum?"

"Beer's fine. But I gotta be going. I gotta date."

"Alright, if you don't want to be sociable," said he old man. "And I accept your apology. I'm sorry I called you a boy."

The Marine nodded at the old man and then got up stiffly from his chair and walked out of the room, turning his shoulders sideways to pass through the waitresses that were standing in the doorway.

The old man sat watching him go, and when he was gone said, "Goddamn punk kid of a jar-head. Fuck him." He turned back around and faced the two Officers who were now getting up from their table. "Can you believe that punk?" he said to them, shaking his head.

The men who looked like Officers smiled and shook their heads, and then they stood and left the room. The waitresses were talking among themselves now, casting dirty looks at the old man every now and then. They had to move out of the doorway to make room for the two Officers, and then they began to drift away in pairs.

"Where's a waitress?" said the old man loudly. He turned to Paul and said, "I'm still gonna buy you a beer. You're more a man than that punk kid was."

Paul just grinned. He felt foolish now, left alone with the old man, and he wanted to leave. It had started to rain outside.

A waitress came into the room, the one with the thick legs, and stood by the old man's table looking bored, and not looking directly at the old man. "Bring me a couple fresh beers, lady," he said.

Paul lit a cigarette and then drank down the rest of his first beer. There was quite a lot of it, because he hadn't drunk any since the girl had ran out of the room.

The old man had taken out his bottle again and was drinking from it. He held the bottle high with the neck in his mouth and took long slow swallows from it. Paul counted six swallows before the old man took the bottle down and screwed the cap back on. Paul could see that his eyes had watered up a little.

Now the old man looked at Paul and said, "I coulda killed that punk, you know. You know that, don't you?"

"Sure," said Paul.

"Well, I could have. Except I didn't want to leave the bottle. Could of cut him up real good."

Paul nodded. "Here come the beers," he said.

The waitress brought the two beers and put them down on the table in front of the old man. "One of them is for my friend there," he told her. The waitress brought one of the beers over to Paul and put it down without looking at him. Then she went back to the old man and held out her hand. He gave her the six Pesos, one of them in coins, and she stood counting it carefully before she left.

"Thanks for the beer," said Paul.

"Drink up," said the old man. "Here's to you." The old man drank his beer from the bottle and a little of it ran down his chin. He put the bottle down and wiped this away with the back of his bony hand. "I coulda cut that boy up real good," he said. "With just my hands see, not a knife." He held up his hands for Paul to see. "Spent most of my life at sea, and I know how to hit a man so it'll cut him real good. Don't need a knife."

"Well, he should mind his own business," said Paul, not really knowing what else to say.

"Listen," said the old man. "That girl is my own daughter. You believe that? Well, she is. I didn't want to broadcast it, you know. She's a whore just like her own mother."

"Oh," said Paul.

"Been looking for her mother, see. Ain't seen her mother in a year or more. Think she is shacked up with a cop up in Angeles City. Fact is, I know it. And I wanna find her so I can kill her. Kill her and the fucking cop too."

Paul did not know what to say.

"It's legal in this country, you know. You can kill your wife and whoever she's with if you catch 'em when they're together cheatin'. Think of that! A cop and my wife, all in one, and maybe a day or two in a cell waiting for the hearing to pay for it!" He laughed, almost a giggle.

"I guess that would be something," said Paul.

"Damn right it would be," said the old man. "You sure you don't want a drink of this bottle now?"

"No thanks. The beer's fine."

"Not much of a drinker, eh?"

"I guess not."

"Well, it ain't nothing to be ashamed of. At least you didn't go sticking your nose in my business a while ago."

Paul smiled.

"Damn jar-head. Could of cut him real good. Woulda too, except of having to leave the bottle. When you get to be my age, it's hard enough to get the damn bottle in the first place, without running off and leaving it alone. You see that, don't you?"

"Sure," said Paul. "Sure."

"Well, I'm going to get out of here. See where that damn girl went." He finished his beer and rose, tucking his paper bag under his arm. "Be seeing ya, son," he said.

"Yeah," said Paul. "Thanks for the beer."

The old man waved his arm at Paul as he walked out the doorway in his shower shoes.

CHAPTER 20

Now it was the afternoon of the third day and Paul Sutton sat with Mar in the room in the house on the green hill behind the town. It was very warm in the early afternoon and Paul sat on the edge of the bed with his shirt open letting the air from the electric fan that sat on floor blow over him. But he could not feel the wind the large fan was making, nor did he feel the sticky heat of the afternoon. The rain still came steadily down outside, and there was only darkness.

He had waited as long as he could wait to come to the house. He had slept until noon the day before, after drinking too much the first night in the Sherry Club, and then he had gone down and waited many hours first in Kong's restaurant, and then in Ding's, sitting alone and drinking beers. It had rained most of that second day, a steady pouring rain that flooded the streets with red mud. Today he had waited as long as he could stand it to come out to the house to see if Rosie had come back from Manila. He had been putting it off, he told himself, because he didn't like the thought of her smelling the beer on his breath.

But now he sat alone with Mar in her room, and the waiting was finally over.

A newspaper lay on the bed between Paul and Mar, and if it had been an English newspaper Paul might have read it, but he could not read *Tagalog*.

But he did not have to read the newspaper to know what it said. The front page had a color photo of a Victory Liner laying twisted and broken on its side.

Mar was not making any sound as she cried. She sat on the bed with her knees together and her hands clasped over her knees and stared across the room to where the clothes hung. More than half of the wall was covered by the dresses and skirts and blouses and pants that were hung there. Paul knew that many of the clothes belonged to Rosie. Margaret sat on the edge of the bed with her eyes open and looking in the direction of the clothes and the tears ran down her brown face like the rain on the window behind her.

Paul watched her crying and thought that she would probably like him to leave now. He thought she looked ugly crying. Her eyes blinked against the tears helplessly now and then, but still she made no sound.

"I'd better go." His voice did not feel like his own as he spoke. It felt as if he hadn't used it for a long time.

Mar looked at him and her face looked dull and empty and old. As she looked at him her mouth began to turn down and to tighten and a low sound started deep within her. Then she was against his lap with her face down and she was talking fast between the sobs, in her own language, the words coming fast and blurred by wetness, and Paul was holding her head with both of his hands. Her face felt hot and her words hit against his thigh wetly. Then after a while she was quiet and Paul held her head in his lap with her short soft thick black hair in his hands and said, "Cry if you want." He felt stupid saying it.

She moved her head back and sat up and looked at him with the redness of her eyes and the wrinkles from pressing her face against him and shook her head. Paul said, "It was just the rain Mar. It was the storm."

Mar looked away, rubbing her face with her hands.

It was just the fucking bus going off the road in the rain and turning over in the ditch, thought Paul. There was no meaning to any of it. It wasn't just that *she* had a sister waiting for her. No. And a mother and a young brother to leave behind. No. It wasn't anything to do with those things, and it wasn't anything to do with him waiting for her either. Waiting here, and her not even knowing. It wasn't who she was, and it was not her being only twenty-eight years old. No tears came to him. But he knew that this was all his fault. No tears, but his throat felt too tight. He almost couldn't breathe.

Maybe the driver drove a little too fast in the rain and didn't see the wash-out and suddenly in the darkness the bus turned over. Yes, it was only the dreadful weather and the fuel still burning in the rain and maybe too many people on the bus. There was no meaning in any of that. But if he had only married Rosie two years before and taken her home, like so many other sailors had done, she would be alive right now. If he had only been patient with her, given her a chance. If he had only asked. He knew he would never forgive his indecision. He was a fool.

Mar said, "I must go to Manila right away. My mother will be taking Rosie back to Tarlac province where our grand-parents live. She will be buried there."

"I will hire a taxi and I will take you," said Paul.

"What will you do then?"

Paul shrugged.

"My sister loved you," said Mar.

"I would like to have one of the pictures of her."

There were a several professional looking photos of her on the wall of the room. There was one black and white print that was a close-up of Rosie smiling with her hair tied back with no visible make-up, her head turned a little so that it looked as if she had not been aware that a photo was being taken, and it was this one that Paul wanted.

"Any of them," said Margaret.

Paul rose and took down the framed photo from where it hung on the wall and he opened his bag and put it inside on top of the softness of a folded blue shirt.

THE END

Made in the USA
San Bernardino, CA
17 August 2018